The world is not made of atoms.
It is made of the stories we tell about atoms.

Copyright © 2016 Nicholas C. Rossis. All rights reserved.
Illustration by Dimitris Fousekis. Copyright © 2014 Dimitris Fousekis. All rights reserved.
Cover by Alexios Saskalidis, 187designz.deviantart.com. All rights reserved.
ISBN: 978-1537566979
This is an original work of fiction. Any relationship to real people is unintentional and a coincidence.

You're in for a Ride: A Collection of Science Fiction Short Stories

Contents

CONTENTS	3
YOU'RE IN FOR A RIDE: INTRODUCTION	5
YOU'RE IN FOR A RIDE: PART I	7
A CRYSTAL TOO FAR	13
YOU CAN'T FIGHT A PROPHECY	19
HEAVY SITS THE FROWN	47
ROYAL DUTIES	49
SHOOT THE DEVIL *(REDUX)*	53
SHH—THE BABY'S SLEEPING	71
YOU'RE IN FOR A RIDE: PART II	81
BONUS STORIES	89
WHAT'S IN A NAME?	91
LITTLE STAR CORVETTE	99
FOR THE LAST TIME!	111
A NOTE FROM THE AUTHOR	125
ABOUT THE AUTHOR	127
ACKNOWLEDGMENTS	129
FURTHER NOTES	131

You're in for a Ride: Introduction

The impregnation euphoria is slowly wearing off. I watch my latest victim's body sink into the mud as I wait for the buzzing in my ears to fade away. Soon, darker thoughts fill my head like crawling insects. My gaze darts round the cavernous basement. I count twenty-seven bodies. Twenty-seven possible offspring. That means two, maybe three survivors—if I'm lucky. Not nearly enough. I need at least another one.

I pinch the bridge of my nose, the weight of my responsibilities weighing heavily upon me. The good news is, the building's mine. Has been for centuries. But I need to renovate it, to make sure that no one disturbs us for the next few decades. Until the next cycle.

Even worse, I've only located forty-eight possible hosts this time. Twenty-one had proven incompatible. Twenty-one! I hid their bodies away, but the police have already unearthed thirteen of them. How long before they catch up with me? Even if they don't, how long before there are no compatible hosts left? They used to beg us for our seed. Now they chase us, call us monsters.

How long before mankind discards the last of its forgotten gods?

You're in for a ride: Part I

A man's gotta make a living, so I cruise through the rain, even though I doubt anyone will be crazy enough to be out and about in a night like this. Which is why I almost miss the middle-aged blonde in the red coat, seeking shelter under the bus stop. She flags me down with both hands, flailing her arms up and down.

I stop a few yards down the road, and she yanks the door open and rushes in. The wind pushes a few stray raindrops into the cab, but I don't mind. I'm just happy to get a customer.

She squishes into the warm seat. "Thanks."

I nod a half-greeting, half-question. "Where to?"

She gives me an address in the better part of the city and I repeat it into the cab's autopilot. The car turns left onto an empty street. Blurry neon lights reflect on my windshield as we drive away from the city center. I make myself comfortable. There's really no need for me to be behind the wheel. Just waiting for legislation to catch up with technology. Maybe in a year's time, more likely in a decade or two, cabbies will be obsolete. I'll be obsolete.

What happens next is anyone's guess. I suppose some passengers will prefer having a real human being in the car with them. Who knows—our presence, once not required, may become a luxury only the rich can afford. At least, that's what we cabbies tell ourselves.

I shake my head to chase away chilling thoughts, and glance at the mirror. She pushes her lipstick against her lips, then shoves it back into her bag and smacks cherry lips together. Her mouth looks ready to break into an easy smile. I like that. Then I notice her jittery gaze darting around the empty, showery streets.

My brow furrows. "Everything all right?"

She lets out a nervous chuckle. "Yes, it's just…" There's that easy smile. A bit on the nervous side, but cute on her. "With everything that's been going on…"

She doesn't finish her sentence. Doesn't need to. We've all heard the news. They'd found another one of the Phantom's victims last night. "What's that, twelve?"

She shakes her head. "Thirteen. Assuming they've found them all."

Thirteen dead in as many months. The police, clueless. Each victim, mummified. Drained of life. It only took the Phantom a few minutes, the coroner had said. How, no one knows.

Comedy clubs roar with laughter as comedians joke about the return of the Mummy. At night's end, though, when the doors open and I pick up tipsy patrons, fear hangs over them like a putrid overcoat.

"Looks like he only strikes once a month," I console her. "We should be safe until next month."

Her lips tug upwards again. "I guess."

I like her smile. Half bitter, half joyful. Would love to promise her she'll be safe. But how can I?

"I heard about a professor in the news," she says. "He claims it's an ancient species. One that hibernates for hundreds of years. They were once worshipped as gods, he said. They'll eat their fill, then return to their slumber."

I let out a nervous laugh. "Does he know why?"

Her smile evaporates. "He speculates they need our life force—*chi*, he called it—to survive."

"Some imagination he has."

"I don't know." She purses her lips. "He sounded pretty convincing. Said he's already unearthed enough evidence to go public. He's close to getting final proof."

"Sounds like a nut job to me," I mutter. "Have you even seen him?"

"I don't think anyone has." She chuckles. "He's about as hard-to-find as the Phantom himself."

We spend the rest of the short ride in awkward silence. That professor and his theories have soured my mood, and the empty streets unnerve me. Not even joyriders—the suicidal idiots who find driving thrilling and race the streets at night with disengaged autopilots. Even they have stayed inside on a night like this.

When the cab pulls over at the curb, she opens her purse and pulls out her cell. It blips as she makes a quick pass over the dongle. I check the transaction. It includes a healthy tip. I beam her my warmest smile. "Have a lovely night, ma'am."

"You too," she says and walks into the rain and out of my life.

My head slumps against my headrest. I watch her through the mirror pull her collar over her head and rush toward a well-kept house. The kind with the manicured lawn. She probably has a family waiting for her. Husband and three-point-five kids. And a flamingo in the backyard.

I swallow a yawn, then remember there's no one around and let it out in the open, not even bothering to cover my mouth. A quick glance at the dashboard tells me it's been sixteen hours now. Way too long a shift, even if I've spent most of it sitting comfortably. I instruct the cab to drive itself to the nearest train station. Maybe I can catch one last fare before calling it a day.

The sound of the rain drumming against the car and the swish of the wipers lull me to sleep. I do my best to keep my eyes open as the car drives through the vacant streets, but as soon as the cab comes to a gentle stop next to the train station sign, I stretch my hands and put them behind my head. Then, I shut my eyes and drift into an uneasy sleep, filled with strange dreams...

A Crystal Too Far

The sergeant wipes thick beads of sweat from his brow with fingers trembling with exhaustion. "It's useless, sir. There's no way we can get to the crystals in time."

The colony delegate—a member of the royal court, no less—glares at the alien force field separating them from their objective. "And you're sure there's no opening?"

"My men have searched every inch of it. There seems to be no way in or out. Just a groove at the top. When we first discovered it, everyone thought we'd cracked it. But it's sealed. Won't budge an inch." His face twitches. "All of our attempts to enter have been in vain."

"How about *making* an opening? What have you tried so far?"

"Everything we can think of," the man says with a resigned sigh. "Chemicals. Brute force. Private Jenkins here even tried chewing through." He points at a man massaging his swollen jaw.

The delegate spits on the ground. "I don't need to tell you how badly the colony needs those crystals. You have no idea how low our stockpile is by now. We may not survive the winter without them—and spring is still a long time away."

The sergeant's face drops even further. "Yes, sir." He rubs the back of his head for a few awkward moments. "Your orders?"

The delegate casts him a distressed glance, then starts pacing back and forth, mumbling. He only pauses twice: once to curse at the transparent material that seems to be mocking them, and once to curse at the aliens who have placed it there. The all-powerful creatures who have built their fortress next to the colony, paying no attention to its inhabitants and their needs. The enigmatic neighbors have brought much-needed supplies with them, but have steadfastly refused to share—or even acknowledge the colony's continuous pleas for cooperation.

The first delegation had been ignored. The second, stomped on. Whether on purpose or by accident was the subject of much heated debate in the colony. Whichever it was, it had led to this ill-advised attempt at thievery.

"Let's face it, sir," the sergeant whispers once the man runs out of swearwords, "the creatures have won this round."

"Impossible," the man snaps at him. "We have the fiercest arsenals of weapons. We have conquered every corner of this planet. We have brains *and* brawn. There *must* be a way." The delegate stops pacing and whirls around. "What about digging underneath? How far below the ground does the barrier go?"

The sergeant stomps one foot to emphasize the ground's stiffness. "It stops at the surface, but the ground isn't the usual soil one might expect. We've never seen anything like it. Our diggers' best estimate is that it'd take us months to break through."

"By which time the crystals will be gone." The delegate explodes in a fresh barrage of curses, this time shaking his fist at the soaring barrier. He freezes in the middle of a particularly nasty—and unlikely—accusation involving the alien who had invented those hellish materials, certain members of his family, and a cucumber. His eyes light up. "We lift it."

The sergeant presses his lips together and examines his hands, rubbing out an invisible smudge from his palm. "Already tried it. No use. We couldn't move it an inch. Even with our entire colony pushing, it won't budge." He discreetly wipes the delegate's spittle from his cheek as the man starts screaming more obscenities at the obstacle.

Finally, the man hangs his head in defeat and hunches over, placing his hands on his lap. "Who will inform the court?"

The sergeant and a dozen privates behind him all take an involuntary step backwards. No one speaks a word.

The delegate looks at them with dark eyes. "Who will inform the court?" he repeats in a low voice. After a moment of awkward silence, he shakes his head and straightens his back. "Very well. You may return to the colony. But we leave behind sentries. As many men as you can spare. Sooner or later, the creatures will need their crystals. I want to know the moment that happens." A glimmer of hope shines in his eyes. "Maybe they'll forget to drop the force field. Or they'll leave an opening unguarded. Who knows? Perhaps we'll get lucky."

As the sergeant starts barking orders, the delegate stares with greedy eyes at the amazing sight of a whole mountain of energy crystals, a mere hand's reach away. "One way or another, we'll get our hands on you," he whispers. "That's a promise."

***

The old woman reaches for the tea cup and clicks her tongue. "Where is my head?" She turns to the young man sitting opposite to her. "Be a dear and fetch me some sugar, will you, darling? It's on the kitchen top."

The man pushes back his chair and stands up. "Of course, Auntie."

"Be sure to close the lid," she shouts after him as he walks into the kitchen. "The ants around here have gotten a bit... antsy lately." She chuckles at her own joke.

"Yes, Auntie," he shouts from the kitchen. He returns a moment later holding a large glass jar in his hands. "You weren't lying about those ants. There's at least a dozen of them on the kitchen top. It almost looks like they're guarding the sugar cubes." He pushes the ornate silver tray covering half the table a few inches to the side and places the jar next to the steaming teacups. "You should get an exterminator."

She gently smacks his hand. "That's a terrible thing to say. They have as much right to be here as you and me." She lifts the lid and skillfully picks a cube with a fine silver tong. The sugar cube splashes into the hot tea and immediately starts melting. "As penance, you'll leave a cube outside for them when you take the jar back," she says as she lifts the cup and stirs her tea.

The young man chuckles and glances at the kitchen. "Well, that should make a few ants very happy."

You Can't Fight a Prophecy

"You can't fight a prophecy," the wrinkly shaman says and gives me a toothless grin. The shrug accompanying his words shakes the feathers around his neck, making him look like a frail old bird trying to give flight.

Fight it? I don't even understand it.

"What's he say, Doc?" the large boulder of a man standing behind me asks. His camouflaged face and broad shoulders make him look like one of the GI cartoons I used to watch as a kid. Long before the men came in the middle of the night to drag me across half the continent to this forsaken place. *For your country*, they had said. Then, why do they look like mercenaries instead of regular troops? Still, the money they dangled wasn't bad. Heck, it was a small fortune. And it's not like I had something better to do with my life. Not since I opened my drunken, big mouth and told everyone at the Christmas party about the Dean and his secretary. Now, no university would touch me with a ten-foot barge pole.

I let out a mental sigh and draw a crumpled red bandana from my back pocket. I wipe enough sweat from my forehead to fill half a bucket. I haven't been in the jungle in over twenty years. How I survived that first field trip is beyond me. Then again, I *was* twenty years younger. Surprisingly enough, I remember the tribe's language fairly well. A dry chuckle escapes my lips. *Much good that's done me. A failed academic turned unlikely jungle hero.*

I swat away a mosquito eager to stab my neck with its straw-like proboscis and notice GI Joe behind me, still waiting for my answer. "Oh, right," I say. "Sorry. Our chopper has him all worked up. He thinks it's a sign."

GI Joe's gaze measures up the ancient shaman sitting upon a thick layer of leaves. Naked, bony legs protrude under a beige loincloth; the only garment on him. Tattoos and scars cover his skin. Painted red lines cross his wrinkled face. Strange how the various bugs seem to ignore him. Instead, they focus on me, even though I've practically showered from head to toe with stinky bug repellant. "A sign?"

I scratch my chin. "Apparently there's some prophecy. An iron bird's children will wake an ancient god, who will destroy the world. Or something like that. It's all very apocalyptic, really."

The captain's face darkens. He glances behind us. A dozen men in camouflage have spread around our helicopter, assault rifles at the ready. "Are we in danger?"

I shake my head emphatically. "No, no, the natives don't care either way. Listen." I turn my attention back to the old shaman. "Will you help us?" I ask in his language. The tongue-twisting words sound like a typewriter, wrapped in tinfoil, falling down the stairs.

His laugh is throaty and cheerful. He clicks his tongue, as if scolding me for my naivety. "If the gods wish you to find your friend, no one can stop you," he says in a rapid series of guttural sounds, like the typewriter was just crashed by a steamroller. "If they don't, no one can help you. Either way, you don't need me." I translate for GI Joe behind me and he mumbles something under his breath.

"Does he know where the rebels are keeping him?" he asks.

I repeat the question to the shaman. He cocks his head for a moment as if listening to the wind, then nods. I take out a map and notice the bemused glint in the old man's eyes. *He's probably never seen paper*, I remind myself. Hell, he hadn't even seen a white man before today. I fold the map away. A thin smile tugs at his lips, followed by a lot of pointing and a burst of words. I hastily draw my pen and scribble down instructions. A forked river. A lake. A snaked wall. Twin mountains. He points behind me. I follow his gaze and see two peaks behind us, barely peeking over the thick canopy of the jungle.

I thank him and unfold the map again. GI Joe looks over my shoulder. I point to an area in the south. "From what I can tell, we need to follow the river farther south. Whenever we come across a fork, we stay on the left. We will end up at a lake. A path leads from its far end to a ridge between those two mountains"—I use my thumb to point behind us—"then we hit something he calls a snaked wall. Or snake wall. Or the wall of snakes?" I scratch my unshaved chin. "It might be a ruined temple. Or some natural phenomenon. I guess we'll know it when we see it."

"Not we, Doc," the gruff man says. "You're staying here."

I almost let out a relieved sigh, then my face drops. "I'd love to. But what if you get lost? Or if you hit a snag? Maybe you meet some other tribe and you need to communicate." I shake my head. "I'm as good a guide as anyone you can find around here. You need me."

He purses his lips, then nods. "Very well. But at the first sign of trouble, you hide."

I chortle. "Don't need to tell me twice."

He turns to his men. "Prepare the dinghies," he barks and two dozen men scramble to their feet.

Within seconds, they are busy loading a pair of huge dinghies with more ammo and supplies than I thought any boat made of rubber could ever hold.

"Why don't we take the chopper?" I ask.

"No place to land for miles," GI Joe explains. "The forest is too thick in the south. Besides, they'll hear us coming. We can't risk them killing the... asset."

Asset. The brief pause and the way he spoke the word suggests a strange affection—even reverence—for the man we've come to rescue. Is he the one the prophecy refers to? Unless, of course, the shaman meant me. Am *I* destined to raise some sort of god? My mouth twitches in frustration. *How can I fight a prophecy I don't even understand?*

Despite the stifling heat, the academic in me is intrigued. All sorts of information gathered during my studies bubble to my head. I open my mouth to further question the ancient shaman, but GI Joe yanks me to my feet.

"Are you coming, or what?" he growls.

His men have already loaded up the dinghies and are finding their places inside. I follow GI Joe and he shoves me into the nearest boat. I find myself squeezed between a tall man made of granite and a stubby one made of ebony, with a face scarred by fire. They grunt in response to my greeting. GI Joe pushes our dinghy into the river. Ebony's hand finds the engine and jolts it to life. The boat bounces forward and seesaws into the river for a moment, then its movement becomes smooth and we stroll along its course.

Every now and then, a Caiman fixes his reptilian eye on us, watching us go by. A distinctive coughing sound alerts me to an arapaima fish emerging for air. This one is half as long as our dinghy. I make sure that all my limbs are safely inside.

"What's so important about this guy, anyway?" I ask Ebony.

"We'd give our lives for him," he whispers. His scarred face burns with a devotion I've never seen before.

"Why?" I blurt out.

Granite scowls at Ebony, who presses his thick lips together. No answer comes.

We ride in awkward silence until we reach a fork in the river. A fallen tree cuts off the left branch. As the two dinghies lumber around it, movement in a limb catches my eye. When I find myself staring into the eyes of an anaconda, I swallow. Its spotty skin makes it almost invisible among the thick leaves, but it must be around twenty feet long and thicker than Granite's thigh. Granite follows my gaze and his whole body jerks. He reaches for his sidearm, but GI Joe shoots him a warning glare and shakes his head. Reluctantly, Granite draws a long breath. His eyes never leave the limb until we're far enough for him to relax his grip on his gun.

"Snakes," he mutters under his breath. "I hate snakes."

"Well, we *are* in a jungle." My words sound more cheerful than I intended. I am rewarded with a poisonous side glance.

I shrug it off and lower my sweaty hat to my eyes. The engine's murmur and the soft bobbing of the boat make me drowsy. My eyes grow heavy, and I drift into an uneasy sleep.

A shove jerks me awake. "We're here," someone whispers in my ear.

I blink to clear cobwebs from my eyes. Granite is towering over me. Behind him, the sun is setting fast, as if anxious to get home after a busy day. I glance around. We have arrived at the edge of a large lake. Slivers of orange-hued sunlight slice through the green canopy overhead and leave its warm glow here and there. The men secure the dinghies and start pulling the crates out. I yawn and stretch. My limbs feel creaky and sore.

"We walk the rest of the way," Granite says and throws a backpack to me.

I catch it with an audible *oomph* that earns me a contemptuous smirk. I ignore him and sling the backpack around my shoulder before jumping out. With a loud *squelch*, my legs sink almost to the knees in sludge. I cringe and yank one leg from the mud's greedy pull. "Pretty soon, it'll be too dark to see anything," I say as I flick away thirsty leeches from my pants. "We should make camp here and leave in the morning."

He points to something like binoculars hanging around his neck, then reaches into a crate and pulls out a similar set. He throws them at me. I catch them just before they land in the muddy waters. *Can't this guy ever pass something like a normal human being?* I imagine him at a dinner table, throwing saltshakers and bottles of wine to his guests, and almost chuckle.

"Nice catch," he says, his voice thick with irony.

The first thing crossing my mind is something about his mother and her marital status at the time of his conception. One look at his bulging muscles has me swallow my words. Instead, I finally manage to free both my legs from their muddy prison and shuffle over to harder ground. "What are these, night goggles?" I ask.

"See for yourself," he says and points at a switch at their top.

I place the goggles in front of my eyes and he flips the switch. The dusky forest turns an eerie green. He pushes a lever back and forth. The image zooms in and out in rapid succession, until my stomach feels queasy.

"It's not *that* dark," GI Joe sniggers as he passes us.

Granite's laugh burns my ears. *Jerks.*

I push Granite's fingers away and tear the goggles from my eyes. It takes a minute or two for my nausea to subside. In the meantime, the soldiers have emptied the dinghies.

We make our way into the forest and clear a path. Soon, I find myself in the middle of a long column, a dozen guys before me, and another behind. Before long, I'm panting, too tired to look at anything but Ebony's boots right ahead. Their rise and fall is hypnotic. Up, down. Up, down. I thank my lucky stars for the nap I had earlier.

Half an hour later, my whole chest burns with every breath. Every muscle aches. Thick sweat covers every inch of my body. The rough terrain is harder to traverse than I remembered. I sigh with relief when Ebony stops. He motions for me to put my goggles on. Like before, I need a moment before I get used to my eerie green surroundings.

Granite runs down the column to fetch me. He motions for me to follow him and leads me to a vine-covered stone wall. It's so ancient, the ground has swallowed most of it. Whatever's left barely reaches to my waist. From the old man's words, I expect it to snake through the jungle. Instead, it runs in a straight line, cutting us off. Etched snakes, almost erased by time, meander through its surface. Granite notices them and draws a sharp breath. I almost smile.

"Now what?" GI Joe asks me.

"Umm..." I scratch my chin. The old man was not exactly a fan of specifics. "I think we're meant to go around it. He warned against crossing it. The whole area here is taboo."

"What about the rebels?" Granite asks. "Where are they?"

"Right past this area. If we keep climbing, we'll reach the top. The camp should be below us."

The two men exchange a loaded glance. Granite nods and disappears into the night to inform the others.

"You wait here," GI Joe says.

"Again, that'd be fine with me," I say. "But what if the old man has it wrong? The camp may be an hour or a day away. Or even a week, for all we know."

His cold stare gives me the creeps. "Very well," he says after a while. He turns to Granite, who has just reappeared behind us, and points his chin at me. "You, watch him."

"Yes, boss," Granite says and motions for me to fall behind him.

We keep the wall to our left and continue our ascent. The jungle is alive with sound even at night—except for the area surrounded by the wall. No birds, no frogs, no crickets. Just a chill that sends cold shivers down my back, despite the still simmering heat. Granite must have felt it too, because he takes a few steps away from the wall and into the jungle. I'm more than happy to follow him.

It doesn't take long to circumvent the wall. It continues in what appears to be a perfect rectangle. We clear a path parallel to it until we leave that whole area behind us. Not a moment too soon, either.

After about an hour, we reach the brow of the ridge. True to the old man's word, we spot lights below. Through the goggles, they burn like stars in a cloudless night. My limbs feel numb by now and my hands shake. On the other hand, only a fine sheen of sweat on Granite's face shows any effort on his part.

GI Joe motions us to lie low. I drop to all fours and use the goggles to zoom in. Below us lies some kind of encampment, surrounded by wooden walls. For some reason, crosses stand on each corner. They look constructed in a hurry, out of fallen tree trunks. Words and symbols I can't make out are etched on the peeling barks.

I tilt the goggles to study the wall. A single entrance leads in and out. Two soldiers guard it. Another four patrol the perimeter. There is a makeshift tower with a searchlight at one corner, with a bored-looking soldier manning a machinegun. Yet another cross rises over him.

I make out four—no, five—buildings including the toilets at the camp's corner. The smallest building sits smack in the middle of the clearing. Six men guard it; one at each corner, and another two at its entrance. I assume that's the jail where they keep the prisoner. More crosses line the walls, hastily nailed to each of the walls and on the door.

Right on cue, the door gives up a wide yawn and a broad-shouldered young man leans into the gap. Two guards raise nervous rifles to stop him from stepping outside. I expect him to go straight back, but he just stands there, a mocking grin dividing his handsome, angular face. *He's the prisoner?* I expected a roughed up, terrified, white-haired man. Instead, I see an athletic man in his early thirties, wearing an impeccable silk suit that has to be tailor-made. His every move carries an unmistakable air of authority, as if the guards were, in fact, the prisoners here.

Thick beads of sweat rush down my back, thanks to the humid heat. My hair clings to my head under my soggy hat. My clothes are muddy and torn. But the prisoner—he looks like he's been having drinks at an air-conditioned, five-star hotel bar. Not a hair on his perfect head is out of place. He tugs at a gold, serpent-shaped cufflink and straightens the snow-white sleeve of his shirt. As if feeling my gaze on him, he lifts his chin and stares right at me, a smug smile on his face. Then, he winks.

I let out an audible gasp. "Who *is* this guy?" I ask Granite.

"Not your concern," he growls as he fixes an earpiece to his ear. He taps it a couple of times, then screws a silencer on the barrel of his rifle in a fluid, methodical motion. A laser scope the size of my arm goes at its top. He fishes an upturned cross from his khaki T-shirt and kisses it.

I watch, mesmerized, the silver amulet as he shoves it back down on his hairy chest. The cross's horizontal bar is so low, it almost looks like an upside-down T. "That's the wrong side up," I blurt out, and immediately scold myself. *Nice, oh master of the obvious. Argue with the guy with the rifle.*

"Just the way it should be," he says absentmindedly as he removes his goggles. He fixes his eye at the scope's end and points the rifle at the guards. "Check," he murmurs. I realize he's responding to some inaudible command, and wish I, too, could hear what was going on.

"How can you be sure you'll hit the guards from so far away?" There is no way they can hear us, but I still find myself whispering.

"These are special bullets," he says. "They have a microchip, like a tiny computer. All you need to do is fix them on the target. The chip takes care of the rest."

These are more words than I've heard him utter during the entire journey. His face beams with so much pride, I wonder if he designed the weapon himself. There is warmth in his voice, as if talking about a loved one. His fingers stroke the barrel of the rifle with genuine affection. I don't need to be a career guide to know this is a man in love with his job.

He raises a finger to stop any further questions. "Check," he repeats, and squeezes the trigger.

I expect a bright flash and *pop*, like in the movies. But there's not even a flicker or a glow, and instead of the pop, I hear a low *thud*, like a hammer hitting the ground. The noise is displaced, coming from all around us. A puff of smoke rises from the thick silencer. I turn my attention back to the camp. All the guards surrounding the jail are dead. So are the two soldiers guarding the entrance. A stunned expression mars their faces, as if some vengeful deity had snuffed all life out of them with a simple snap of his fingers.

A thin line of men approach the camp from the outside. One of them scales the wall and disappears. Moments later, the gate opens and the rest of them sneak inside.

Before they have a chance to reach the jail, the door to the toilets opens and a lone soldier breaks the threshold, still zipping up. Spotting his dead companions, he lets out a piercing shriek. He pulls a pistol from a waist holster and fires at the men crossing the courtyard as his trousers pool around his ankles. A bullet sends him crashing back into the toilet, but the damage is done. An alarm blares. With so many crosses around, I half-expect it to blare Gregorian chants, but no, this is an old-fashioned high-pitched alarm. The searchlight catches our men. They scurry to take cover behind anything they can find—crates and barrels mostly. GI Joe and Ebony hide behind a dilapidated truck.

An endless stream of guards rushes out of all four buildings. Rapid gunfire breaks the stillness of the jungle night. Pained screams send chills down my spine until the machinegun's dry *ack-ack-ack* drowns out all other noises.

A bright light blinds me momentarily. I duck for cover as an explosion rocks the ground. Debris lands on my head. Granite lets out a curse and drops his rifle. Blood seeps out of his massive chest. He clenches his jaw in pain and moans.

I rush to his side and check his wound. Shrapnel has hit him, but his body armor has absorbed most of it. He has multiple small cuts that don't worry me, and a deep wound on his shoulder that does. "You'll be fine," I say as I empty a can of blood-stopping foam on the wound. Like magic, the crimson flow slows from a river to a trickle. The painkillers in the foam must be working, because his face relaxes.

"Thanks, Doc," he says and groans.

"Don't mention it," I say and turn my attention back to the camp.

The tower lies in ruins, but several of our men are lying dead. Under heavy fire, GI Joe and Ebony zigzag between the buildings until they reach the jail. They tear down the door and throw it to the side. The prisoner casually tugs his other cufflink before following them back to the camp entrance. His stride is confident. When Ebony throws his hands in the air and drops to the ground, the prisoner frowns and wipes blood droplets from his jacket. GI Joe shoves him through the gate and turns around to return fire. Bullets rip through his chest. They must be armor-piercing, because he drops to the ground like a lead mannequin. He never gets up.

I search for the prisoner, but he's disappeared. I take cover as another series of explosions covers me with branches and mud. My ears ring, which is probably why I don't hear the young man approach.

"Good evening, gentlemen."

I jump out of my skin. His voice is deep and poised. For some reason, he sounds… amused? The guy hasn't even broken a sweat.

"We should get out of here, sir," Granite says and bows his head with respect.

The freed prisoner nods. I place an arm around Granite to help him to his feet. We hurry back down the slope. Behind us, sporadic gunfire and booming explosions suggest the remnants of our force are covering our getaway. We descend as fast as we can until we reach the wall. Keeping it to my right, I start the detour around it.

"What are you doing?" the young man asks. "It's just a knee wall. Surely you can scale it?"

"It's taboo," I say, then notice Granite's scolding face. "What?"

"Forgive him, sir," he says. "He doesn't understand."

The young man brushes him off with a dismissive flick of his wrist. "That's fine." A carefree smile parts his lips. "When I'm with you, you needn't worry about a thing."

Try telling that to GI Joe, I think, but decide it's best if I keep my mouth shut.

"Besides," he continues, "this would make a splendid headquarters. Feels right, doesn't it?"

The place gives me the creeps, but I can take a hint. "Whatever," I mumble under my breath and help Granite over the wall. We head straight to the middle of the enclosed area. The ground is moist and muddy, like marshland. Broken pillars jut out of the water like the fossilized bones of prehistoric monsters. I can see no trees within the compound. It's almost like this area doesn't belong to the jungle at all. Above us, the low rumble of thunder echoes. A frown etches my brow. *It was clear a moment ago.*

All my hairs stand on end as we approach a raised stone platform. Some sort of crumbling altar sits at its center. I can't shake the feeling we're being watched.

Granite lets out a sudden yelp and slips right through my hands and into a hole in the ground.

"Granite!" I cry out.

The former prisoner cocks an eyebrow. "That's not his name."

I ignore him and lean over the hole. I hear moans. "We're coming," I shout.

"We are?" the young man asks in surprise.

I glare at him. "We are." I consider jumping after Granite, but have no idea how deep this hole is. Were I with someone else, I might ask them to lower me with a rope. But I have no rope. And I'm sure this guy would just leave me there to rot, anyway. My gaze darts frantically around. I spot stairs right before the altar. They seem to lead down below.

I run to the platform and jump down a stone stairway. The uneven steps are slippery with mud, as I realize when my foot does a funky dance and ends up in front of my face. Letting out a curse, I land flat on my face in stinking stale waters. It takes me a moment to regain my composure. When I do, I notice an impatient hand waiting for me.

I take it and the young man lifts me to my feet as if I were made of straw. There's not a speck on his fine suit. Even Ebony's blood has disappeared. *Who the hell is this guy? The patron saint of drycleaners?*

"Thanks," I mumble and scrunch my nose at my own stench. He stares at me, an amused twinkle in his onyx eyes.

We are standing at the end of a crumbling corridor. Gunshots echo all around us. My head jerks left and right, trying to identify its origins. Long bursts. Then, the curt *pow-pow-pow* of a sidearm.

"This way," he says and marches down the corridor as if he owns the place.

He snaps his fingers and a torch on the stone walls bursts to flames as we pass, blinding me for a moment, and almost giving me a heart attack. "What the..."

Then another torch lights up. And another. I remove my goggles and rub my eyes. We reach a cavernous circular room. Yawning pathways lead away to corridors like the one we just came from, like spokes on a wheel. At its center lies Granite.

"Snakes," he hisses as I dash toward him. "I hate snakes." He turns his handgun at his temple and squeezes the trigger.

My eyes widen. "No!" I vault at him but am too late.

Click.

He stares with dismay at the empty weapon and throws it away. His gaze focuses on something behind me and terror fills his eyes. He lets out an inhuman shriek.

I spin around and my jaw drops. A hulking, growling beast, covered in a crustacean shell is slithering toward us. Four sets of powerful claws snap at us. The lower part of the creature's body is anaconda-like, and over thirty feet in length. Four insectoid eyes glare at us. Twin bat wings unfurl from its back. The whole thing looks designed by a drunken mad geneticist. On acid.

It opens its mouth and a foul stench makes me cover my face with my shirt. The creature raises a claw to strike.

"Not so fast," the young man says and casually steps between us and the beast. "They are with me."

The beast cocks its head, making the writhing tentacles that cover its neck sway sickeningly. It lets out a long snarl.

"Normally, I'd agree with you," the young man says condescendingly, "but, like I said,"—he raises his chin and reveals perfect teeth in a threatening grin—"they're with me. You don't want to mess with another man's property now, do you?"

Property?

The creature growls something back.

"Great Old One, huh?" the young man says, smiling with mock pleasure. "Nice to meet you. They call me the Beast."

"I'm Benny," I mumble, "but everyone calls me Doc." *Did I just say that?*

They both stare at me for a moment, then the monster puts two claws on its waist and snarls something.

"I don't care about no stinkin' prophecy," Beast says, glaring at it, "or how ancient you really are. This is *my* world to destroy." He offers a lopsided grin, like the two sides of his face can't agree on any one particular expression. "You ever heard of the Apocalypse, ol' timer? *Woe to you, Oh Earth and Sea, for the devil sends the Beast with wrath* and all that?" He takes a mock bow. "At your service."

I take a step back, my jaw hanging. *Wait, what?* I'm trying to figure out if he's deluded or worse. Much, much worse. The upturned cross on Granite's chest, the crosses at the encampment—everything makes perfect sense.

Despite the suffocating heat, cold sweat breaks out and covers my shivering body.

The creature roars and stomps its claws against its chest. The whole room quakes. Dirt rains on us from the crumbling ceiling.

Beast sighs theatrically and swats away dust from his shoulders. "Fine. Have it your way." He removes his jacket, folds it neatly, and hands it to me. "Hold this, will you, Doc? This won't take but a moment."

I nod and shuffle away, unable to tear my eyes off of them.

The monster charges at him with a combined attack from all its four claws. Beast cowers and a shimmering light covers him in a crackling red sphere. Sparks fly around him as the shield absorbs the brunt of the attack. For a split second, I swear the young man transforms into a muscular, red-skinned, horned demon, pointy tail and all. A bright red circle with three spokes shines on his forehead, forming three sixes. His eyes burn like amber coals. I blink, and it's a perfect young guy cowering within the red sphere again.

The monster recoils and the shield disappears.

Beast dusts off his lapels with the back of his slim hand. "My turn." He raises his arms, as if pushing against the creature. Flames burst from his palms, encasing the monster. In a split second, it rolls to its side in one swift motion, covering itself within its armored shell. The fire disperses safely around it.

The creature lets out an angry roar and swivels its monstrous tail at us. Beast and I roll safely away, but Granite isn't so lucky. The tail catches him as he's on all fours, trying to get to his feet. He crashes against the far wall with a sickening *crunch*.

I rush to his side.

The light leaves his eyes. "Snakes," he says and spits blood. "I hate..." With a sigh, his body slumps, lifeless, to the ground.

Oh, crap!

"I could take you with one hand," Beast boasts and raises his right arm. This time, a volley of missile-like lightning shoots from his palm. The beast jumps to the ceiling. Two missiles bounce against the thick armor, but most of them miss their mark and end up blowing up part of the far wall. Again, the room quakes and debris rains from above.

Screw this. I'm outta here. I steal one last glance at Granite's dead body and dash off in the direction of the lit torches. Behind me, occasional booms echo, like faraway thunder. I climb the stairs two at a time and burst out and into the night. I drink the air in hungry gulps. Even the stale air of the marshland enclosure feels refreshing after the stench underground.

I place the goggles over my eyes and make my way toward the dinghies. It's downhill on the way back, so I make great time. My only worry is that the remnants of our team will have arrived before me and taken off.

When I finally reach my destination and spot the boats, I let out a cry of relief. My lungs are on fire, but I don't care. I push one of the dinghies into the water and jump inside. I turn the engine on, just as the first rays of the sun make a tentative appearance, sending bands of pink to blend into the dark purple of the horizon. *I've made it.*

In the distance, thunder echoes. Half a dozen toucans take flight as I check the clear sky. No, not thunder. Definitely not thunder.

***

The roar of a helicopter landing interrupts my slumber. I grab the box from under the bed before stepping outside. The sun is barely up as yet another group of mercenaries meets me. Their helicopter has landed among the rest of the choppers, making the tiny village resemble a bustling airport.

That's the good thing about Satanists: they're very persistent, I think as I rub my eyes. "Gentlemen," I say and stifle a yawn.

Yet another version of GI Joe approaches me. This one's even younger than the rest and blond but, apart from that, has the same athletic build and square jaw. "You're Doc?"

"Indeed I am." I raise my hand to avoid a handshake, as they all have an annoying tendency to crush my fingers in their grip. "Welcome. Let me save you some time. As I told your predecessors, you will find what you seek if you head south on the river, take the left branch whenever you find a fork, and continue until you reach a lake. You can land at its far side, where, presumably, you will find an awful lot of dinghies similar to yours." I chuckle. "Forgive me, it's been a few months since I was last there, so I've lost track of just how many they might be. The place probably resembles a busy port by now."

GI Junior shoots me a venomous glare. "Just tell us where to find him."

A distant thunder booms as my friend, the shaman, reaches us. "Judging by the sound," I say, "he's still in the underground temple where I last saw him. Just follow the path from the lake to the brow of the ridge until you meet a snake wall."

"A what?"

"A knee-high wall marked with snake images," I patiently explain, showing with my palm just how tall the wall is. "You'll know when you see it. Besides, the path must be pretty well-trodden by now."

He whips around to leave.

"Wait," I shout. "Two things before you go."

He stops and crosses his big arms before his muscular chest as he faces me.

"First of all, if you go there, you'll die." I speak slowly to make sure he understands. "I'm giving you fair warning, because I don't want your blood on my hands."

He dismisses me with a scoff. "And the second thing?"

I give him my sweetest smile. "My friend and I"—I point to the shaman, who responds with his trademark toothless grin—"have a wager going on. His god against yours. Care to join us?"

"What, his ancient relic of a god?" GI Junior asks and laughs. "I'm in. What's the pot?"

"Last time we checked, it was some fifty grand."

He pulls crumpled banknotes from his pocket and counts them. "Five hundred says we're back within the day."

"Ask your men if they want in on the action."

His lips spread in a cocky grin. "I will. I'll even give your friend his god's head on a pike. As a souvenir."

I take the money with a fake laugh and watch him leave. He spins his finger in the air to gather his men.

"Poor sap. Easiest money ever," I say and open the box. Banknotes fly out. The shaman and I grab them and shove them back inside. "We need a bigger box, buddy," I say in my friend's language. "Maybe we can find one in one of them choppers while GI Junior gets our money." I push the last notes in with my palm and snap the lid shut. "Let me get this back to my hut first." That's the beauty of this place. Banknotes mean to the natives about as much as dead leaves do. I could leave a central bank's worth of cash lying around, and no one would even consider stealing it.

The shaman nods, a sheepish smile on his lips.

The ground shakes under our feet. I lean against the hut's wall. "Whoa. That was a big one. Wonder what those two are up to."

The shaman follows me inside my hut. "How long will they fight?" he asks.

"These guys? Decades. Centuries. Millennia," I say and tuck the box back under my bed. "See, buddy, you were wrong. You *can* fight a prophecy. All you need is another one."

Heavy Sits the Frown

The farm boy setting up the festive decorations steals a look at the castle. Over its palisade, he can make out the mighty king pacing the balcony. The lad stops tying up the ribbons on the maypole for a moment and shelters his eyes from the scorching midday sun, a deep frown between them. He wipes dripping sweat from his brow as his eyes set upon their monarch. His heart fills with envy.

What he wouldn't give to sit upon the keep's massive walls. To not waste his existence in mindless, repetitive chores at the farm all day and pointless drinking with the lads in the evening. To live an important life, to rule the land, or at least sit at the round table where all important decisions are made. To be important.

***

The mighty king takes a break from endless war plans to steal a look at the festive preparations below. In the courtyard, he can make out a handsome lad setting up some ribbons around a maypole. The older man stops pacing the balcony for a moment. He squints, his eyes set upon his subject. Deep lines scar his brow. His heart fills with envy.

What he wouldn't give to be free from the castle's oppressive walls. To not waste his existence worrying where the next threat would come from. To not fear the whispers in the dark, the cloaked dagger, the poison in the wine. To live free, in a simple village or, even better, a distant farm. To toil the fields in the morning and play drinking games with the lads in the evenings. To live a simple life, away from the round table where life and death decisions are made. To be unimportant.

Royal Duties

I know the place is trouble as soon as we pass the twin marble columns and enter the austere palace. Pained cries assault my ears, coming from behind a closed door at the end of an endless corridor. Our footsteps echo on the shiny marble floor until we reach it.

A fresh scream comes from behind the polished mahogany. All my hairs stand on end. I glance at my trusted bodyguard, expecting us to flee. His face drops and he shakes his head. This is a trial I have to go through, his eyes seem to say.

The door creaks open. A listless boy stumbles out, dragged by a red-faced woman. His limbs twitch as if he's a broken mannequin. A puppet with cut strings. I stare with pity at the whimpering kid as they make their way down the long corridor. Then I realize they're headed the right way. Unlike me.

My bodyguard takes my hand and squeezes it. For courage. Is it me, or has the color fled his face? He pushes the door open and we march into a strange, yet vaguely familiar, room. Eerie lights play on the walls. Haunting music fills the room. My gaze studies the walls as I struggle to locate its source. An orange flame of a light catches my eye. It licks the far wall, burning bright over a long bed. Sharp instruments hang above it and next to it. Their shiny, steel surfaces reflect the hellish flame like a hall of mirrors.

Hazy memories fill my head. I've been here before. How long ago, I can't remember. In fact, I can't remember much of anything about it. *What did happen? And who would go to all the trouble of removing my memories?* I swallow, my throat suddenly dry, and consider bolting. But I can't. My bodyguard had made this clear.

An older man is sitting behind an ornate table, scribbling furious notes on a piece of paper. A ghostly light plays on his face, from a large, square lamp in front of him. When he's done, he turns his unwelcome gaze to us. I expected an ogre; I get a wizard instead. His white hair is long and unkempt. It flies behind his ears, making him look like a poor Santa Claus imitation. His dead eyes catch my attention. Made of glass, they hold no expression. They only mirror the strange lights in the room. *How can he even see?*

My skin crawls as he stands up, revealing bright red stains on his white clothes. *Blood?* When he makes his way to us, I fight to stop from running away, back to the safety of the crowded streets. His mouth twitches and he mumbles something unintelligible before grabbing my arm. He picks me up as if I'm made of straw. I let out a cry of protest and glance at my bodyguard. I expect him to spring to action. Instead, he stands still like a flesh statue. The wizard must have put a spell on him.

Panic swells in my chest. I struggle to hide it for a moment, but my lips open on their own and a muffled scream escapes my mouth when I realize we are headed for the bed. The wizard lifts me onto the hard surface and pushes me down. When I protest, he pushes two fingers against my jaw until it relaxes enough for him to empty a small glass bottle into my mouth. He then pushes my jaw closed until I have no option but to swallow. A sickly sweet liquid burns my throat. When his monstrous hands let go of me, I spit out as much as I can. It's not much. I've already swallowed most of it. My gaze darts around the room. I need something to wash away the foul taste, but no water is on offer.

I let out the scream I've been holding in my lungs all this time, in the hope that my bodyguard will break free from the malicious spell and help me. The wizard takes a stunned step back. I try to jump off the bed, but the man leans forward again and pins me down with his outsized hands. I fight with tooth and nail, but he's stronger than me. That's when it hits me. My scream—that's how I fight him.

I let out another, even louder, scream. I expect the man to let go of me long enough for me to make my escape. Instead, he grabs a ceremonial, round dagger and stabs my thigh. Blood soils my skin. My eyes widen in terror. This time, the scream is real. Pain and panic fill me in equal measure. The room spins.

Just as I'm about to collapse, my bodyguard finally frees himself from the spell and springs to action. He dashes to the bed and helps me to my feet. My panic swiftly turns to rage and I shoot a furious glare at him, but gratitude soon replaces my anger. I stumble to the door. He guides me out on quivering legs.

With one hand he pushes the creaking door open, his other arm consoling me. My heart swells at the sight of the exit at the end of the corridor. I can't stop shivering. Sobs shake my body. Tears streak down my cheeks. What madness is this? What did I do to deserve this?

***

"Let me take the little princess outside and I'll be right back," the father says as he takes the wailing little girl into his arms and wipes her eyes with the back of his hand. "Her mother must have arrived by now. She'll take care of her."

"Of course," the pediatrician says before making his way back behind his desk. He sits down and wipes his glasses with a silken piece of cloth. "I have to update her records, anyway. This was her second round of shots, right?" When no one answers him, he looks up, but the two of them have already left. He places his glasses back on his face and stares with dismay at the red smudges soiling his bright white shirt. *That damn pen. On a brand new shirt, too.* He sighs and turns his attention to the computer screen facing him. "I knew I should have become a gynecologist," he mumbles to himself as he taps the keyboard. "These kids all look at me as if I were some kind of monster."

Shoot the Devil (Redux)

"*Papieren,*" a voice barks behind me.

I freeze in my tracks. My heels stop clicking on the pavement. I thought I could sneak into my destination unseen at this late hour, but this city has more eyes than cobblestones. *Act natural*, my instructor's voice whispers in my head. The same thing he's been repeating daily during our six months of ceaseless training.

I turn slowly around, one hand in the air, the other digging into my purse for my battered wallet. Since leather is no longer used in the twenty-second century, this is an heirloom brought along specifically for the purpose. I fish out my pass to hand it over to the impatient hand.

A young man roams his eyes over the length of my body and down my dress. Despite the heavy coat, I feel him stripping me with his eyes. *As if these fabrics weren't bad enough.* I cringe and shut my eyes for a moment. In my head, I rip off the itchy wool dress and stockings and scratch my whole body from head to toe. *I hate the twentieth century.*

"*Papieren, bitte,*" the man corrects himself, making me open my eyes again. A flirty smile is now playing on his lips.

Yech. As he reaches for my papers, two soft pops break the silence of the night, a crying baby in one of the nearby apartments almost drowning them out. His eyes widen. Flirting morphs into shock within a split second. He crashes on the cobblestone pavement before he has a chance to realize what has happened.

I can't stop staring at his clean-shaven face. *God, they're so young,* I think. The countless hours spent training have not prepared me for the stark reality of Nazi Germany. Somehow, I had expected everything to be more cinematic and less... well, less real. That's the problem with time travel; everything is so similar, yet the smallest detail can seem odd.

The copper smell of blood hits my nostrils. It soils the pavement and spreads onto the street. My stomach turns. I bring my fist to my mouth to force down bile.

"Will you just stand there?"

My partner emerges from the shadows to kneel next to the soldier. He presses two fingers to the man's throat. Satisfied that the soldier's heart is no longer pumping, he grabs the body by the shoulders and drags him into a building's entrance. He pauses just long enough to throw me a silver torchlight. "Clean up."

I flip a switch on the device. A pulsing blue light flashes against the stones. I direct it at the blood trail. Within seconds, the light dissolves the clotting blood, leaving behind nothing but a moist smudge that no one will notice.

My partner pulls out a skeleton key and jiggles it into a rusted lock until it clicks softly. We hurry inside a medieval building and shut the door behind us, before slipping into a dark corridor filled with the reassuring stench of boiled cabbage. A baby's plaintive cries attack us from an apartment to my left, followed by a faint argument.

We push the body down a dark staircase and wait until we hear a thump. I use the blue light to clean up red streaks from the wide stones, while my partner hurries down the stairs to hide the body in the basement. It will soon be discovered, but we'll be long gone by then.

I am about to head downstairs to help him when a brown door on the side creaks open to reveal a woman's ancient face. She throws me a stern, suspicious look as I squeeze the torch into my pocket.

"Who are you?" she asks me in German, glancing at the bulge under my breasts.

"A friend…" I rasp in German and cough to clear my clogged throat. "A friend of Dr. Schumann's. He's visiting family in Berlin."

My heart pounds as she takes this in, her eyes never leaving my face. I straighten the hemline of my dress with long, nervous strokes. Finally, she shoots me a venomous look. "Tell him he's late for the rent."

"I will," I promise. Without a word, she slams the door.

I wipe beads of sweat from my brow as my partner emerges from the staircase. "The light." He extends his hand until I hand him the torch. A few moments later, he reappears. "Done. Now, where to?"

I point upstairs and we make our way into Dr. Schumann's apartment. As we climb the stairs, I pull out a dull gray metal cylinder from a hidden pocket in my thick coat. It hisses when I pry it open, expanding into a two-barreled gun. With a soft whir, a laser scope snaps in place at the top, projecting a red dot on the wall across from me. Its comforting weight in my hand helps my breath slow down.

We slink inside and I wrinkle my nose; the apartment reeks of alcohol. I blink for a moment before moving any farther, my eyes still getting used to the low light.

"Greetings, Doctor," my partner says to a still silhouette on an armchair while I hang my coat on a nail by the door.

No reply comes. Like our intel had suggested, Dr. Schumann is lying in his favorite corner of the room, dead as a lanky doornail, the victim of chronic liver failure. His half-open eyes reflect the soft light coming from outside through the dingy, tattered curtains. I pad over to close them, avoiding his lifeless stare.

The soft music coming from the huge radio facing him comes to an abrupt end, followed by a yelling announcer. As my heart skips a beat, I wonder if I should keep it on, then decide that my nerves are too fraught for sudden sounds. I turn the knob, welcoming the ensuing quiet.

A thin beam of pale light cuts through the middle of the tall window overlooking the small plaza where Hitler will arrive in less than an hour. As my partner heads toward it, he trips over an empty bottle and kneels to plonk it onto a table.

I consider turning on a light as he pries the window open to glance outside. Chances are no one will look up, but we have already maxed out our luck for one night, and I don't want to take any risks. I pull the gun out of the coat's pocket and join my partner next to the window. He pulls a nearby chair for me and I sit down, then examine my gun under the streetlamp's soft glow. The laser sight whirs and turns as it calculates distance, a red dot pointing at the ceiling.

"Can you do it?" my partner asks.

I look through the scope and see the magnified vision of two stone columns, a thick, ornate wooden door between them. "Yes." At this range, and with this weapon, even a half-blind man could do it. All I have to do is tag Hitler the moment he appears. The smart bullet will do the rest. Even if I aim at the ceiling, it will fly out the window and explode upon contact with its target.

I take deliberate, slow breaths to calm my nerves. My partner notices this.

"I thought you'd done this before," he says.

"I have. But not for real."

He clicks his tongue. "Sure it was. You blew this bastard's head clean off. I've seen the vid."

I shrug. "And then I came back, and nothing had changed. As per protocol, a time agent stopped me before the timeline could change. They rebooted history and the Nazis went through with their crimes."

"Well, this time it's different." He places a hand on my shoulder, sending goosebumps along my spine. My eyes leave the scope and meet his worried gaze. "Do you want me to do it?"

I push off his hand, annoyed. "I told you, I've done it before. You just focus on your end. Make sure they can't change the timeline back."

"I told you, you got nothing to worry about." He sounds miffed. "I've set up the detour. Instead of the recovery room, we'll end up in time to stop the agent. Besides, it's already played out, hasn't it?"

"I don't know," I confess and bite my lip. "Time travel, paradox fields... It's all a bit too much for me."

He places his hand on my shoulder again and gives me a light squeeze. "All you need to know is that tonight, we make a difference." His voice is now softer.

I say nothing for a few moments. I know it's just nerves, really. He cares for me, or he would never agree to break every oath we took; every rule we'd been taught; every instinct we had. Preservation of the timeline is the number one concern of every time traveler. I still can't believe he has agreed to help me break it. But Hitler has to pay for his crimes. For real, this time.

I return my eye to the scope and lose track of time staring at the twin columns. I jolt when a car speeds into the plaza and four dark-clad men jump out. I instinctively draw back into the room's shadows as they study the surrounding buildings. After a moment, they disappear toward the plaza's four corners, while the driver parks the car under my building. *It won't be long now.*

I rub sweat off my palms and pull a pair of gloves from my pocket. The last thing I want is to have the gun slip through my fingers as I pull the trigger; I only have one chance at this. I stare with disdain at my sweaty, shaking fingers as I push them into their soft constraints.

The sound of more cars screeching outside makes me hurry up, snapping the gloves on my hands. I steal a look outside; three cars have stopped before the City Hall's entrance. I have no idea what the Fuehrer wants there at this late hour; our intel doesn't extend that far. Nor do I need to know, of course. Like countless Jews before me, all I want is a shot at the man who had nearly destroyed my people.

With a flick of my thumb, I switch the laser off and stare down the scope, focusing on the car in the middle. I almost slam the trigger as its door flies open and a bodyguard steps out to glance around, then force myself to sit still, any sudden movement certain to draw attention. When the man steps to the side, holding the door open, I have him in my sights.

The monster who was responsible for millions of deaths springs out of the car with an agility that catches me off guard. I curse silently, flicking the laser sight on with my thumb. A tiny red dot, clearly visible through the scope, dances on the stone steps, trying to lock onto the short man rushing toward the yawning doors of the building. I hold my breath and tag him with the laser until a soft beep confirms the lock.

As if knowing that something is wrong, my target pauses for a moment and his gaze darts around. I squeeze the trigger just as the Fuehrer lifts his head to face my way.

The soft bang is barely perceptible. The breaking of the window, on the other hand, makes me jump. *We should have opened it,* I realize. For a split-second, Hitler's mustached lip quivers at the loud crash as he stares at me, bug eyed, then his head explodes into countless tiny fragments, spraying warm droplets over his stunned bodyguards. Blood flies onto the steps below like swirling scarlet raindrops, baptizing the marble in his blood. The Fuehrer's knees buckle, sending his body to crash against the stone.

Loud yells and shouts shoot from outside. A woman screams as I jump up and bring my hand to my mouth to drown a cackle. I pull back into the safety of the dark apartment. *I did it!* My heart fills with primal joy as my pulse pounds on my temples.

My partner grabs me by the shoulders and kisses me hard on the lips. "We have to go," he says as he breaks the kiss. "Just like we said."

I nod, my head still spinning. A countdown starts in my head; we have to stop Zion from resetting the timeline. Rotating the buckle on my belt to reveal a small indentation, I click it with my finger. The buckle splits open and I press the inconspicuous button inside, before releasing the breath of relief that has caught in my throat.

Normally, we would return straight to the recovery room, while an agent travels back in time to stop us from entering the time machine, thus undoing the assassination. But my partner has set off a different course for us. A detour that will lead us straight into the sphere room. For better or for worse, there will be no going back. Not to the same future, anyway. I clutch my partner's hand and shut my eyelids as the room starts to spin and fade away.

When I crack them open again, I stand in an arched room with a large silver sphere in the middle. My head pounds—one of the unfortunate results of time travel. I almost lose my balance and stumble forward. Thankfully, my partner grabs my arm and steadies me.

Careful, he mouths.

I nod and stare at my feet, waiting for the room to stop spinning. It doesn't help that the room is round, or that a blood red light is flashing over the secured twin doors. At least the walls are a dull, plain gray. Anything more exciting and my lunch would be coloring the concrete floor.

My partner nudges me and nods toward a man in a plain khaki uniform stopping a previous version of us from entering the sphere. A blue beret is sticking from his right shoulder strap, making him our target.

"Right now, you should be recovering," he tells our past versions. "The recording to show you the assassination should be on our server. So, it's time to deactivate the paradox field generator."

I take a step forward and catch my self's eye. She winks at me. I take another step and a wave of nausea hits me. I nod at my partner, who tiptoes to the agent and taps his shoulder. The man's eyes bulge as he spins around and sees us.

"You're not supposed to—" The past version of my partner sneaks up on him and brings his arm around the man's neck. The agent grabs his arm and twists his body in a vain attempt to escape the chokehold. After a few endless moments, he stops flopping and goes limp on my partner's arms with a soft sigh.

I rush to his side as fast as the spinning room lets me. "Did you..."

He shakes his head, panting. "He'll be fine. Just unconscious."

I notice that my self from the past is gaping at us. "Hurry up," I shout and motion toward the sphere's open door. As if snapping from a dream, my past self drags my past partner by the hand and into the sphere. Within a couple of seconds, it blinks out of existence.

"That was easy," I say.

My partner rubs his chin. "Almost *too* easy," he says, just as an alarm starts blaring.

With each blast, my head feels like exploding. I push my hands against my ears. Floodlights snap to life, fixing on our position.

"Now what?" I shout to be heard over the deafening noise.

"Now we wait," my partner shouts back.

The doors to the room burst open. Armed soldiers storm inside. We both raise our arms in the air. I hold my breath and close my eyes. A gentle gust of wind makes me open them again. Our surroundings rapidly turn transparent, like one of those fadeout effects you see in old movies. The guards, too, fade away. They look around them and at each other, their eyes as wide as the floodlights fixed on us. I blink and the room is gone, along with the startled troops.

Instead of the sphere room, we find ourselves inside the blackened end of a hollow crater, towered by the twisted skeletons of ruined buildings, sticking out of the ground like fossilized fingers of some prehistoric monster. Crumbled edifices and broken columns are all that remain of once proud skyscrapers. A light breeze stirs the omnipresent dust and ash. Like gray snowflakes, ash particles dance lazily around us for a moment before settling back down on the ruins.

Above us, constant lightning streaks through a sky thick with leaden clouds. No sun is to be seen. The light coming through has a dull yellow hue, like it's sick and dying. I stop breathing and listen for a sign of life: the tweet of a bird; the barking of a dog; the wailing of a baby. Nothing. Only distant thunders interrupt the eerie silence.

We exchange a baffled look and start climbing out of the hole. I take one step and the soft ground gives way under my feet. My shoe sinks into unsteady pebbles. My partner grabs my arm and helps steady me.

"Thanks," I rasp.

When we finally reach the lip of the crater, I take off my shoes and remove ash and pebbles before putting them back on. My gaze searches the dead city. The crater lies in the middle of a crumbling asphalt street. Rusty cars lie under tons of debris, their occupants long gone. They appear to be really old, like from a century ago. At least.

My partner coughs to clear his throat. "What the hell happened here?"

I rub stinging dust off my eyes. "Are we in the right place?"

He pulls a cell out of his pocket and flicks the screen on. He checks it for a moment, then lifts it in the air and does a slow spin. "No signal of any kind." He puts the device back into his pocket. "But it looks like we're in the right place. Look." He points at the crumbling façade of an ancient building. "Isn't that the church behind our building?"

"Is it?" I study a cracked dome in the distance. The surrounding structure once consisted of high walls and smaller chapels. Now, all that remains is that cleft dome and a collapsing bell tower, perching perilously next to it. "Or, at least, what remains of it," I mumble.

"If there's one place bound to have records, that has to be a church."

We make our way to the complex. Neither of us speaks. The cold numbs my hands and feet. I reach and grab his hand with mine. He squeezes it at first, then his hand slips from beneath my fingers and hangs limp by his side. I mimic him and we walk that way until we reach a tall stone rampart. Without a word, he points at an opening where the wall has given way. We enter a courtyard filled with broken columns. Normally bustling with activity and pilgrims, there is not a soul to be found. A chill runs across my spine and I squeeze my coat against me, realizing I'm still wearing the same clothes I wore when I shot Hitler. For some reason, the thought annoys me and I speed up.

"Over here," he says and points at a metal door. Rusted hinges keep it closed.

I grasp the door handle and pull. It creaks and the door opens an inch with an agonized moan. "Come help me, will you?"

He rushes to my side. I search his face, but he avoids my gaze and grabs the handle. "On three," he says.

"One, two..." I put all my weight and pull.

Crack! The top hinges give way. The door jerks open, like a half-opened tin lid. The clamor echoes through the courtyard. I half-wish, half-dread seeing another human being, but no one appears.

The interior is pitch black and smells of decay. It is a rancid smell that makes me twitch my nose. My partner flicks a switch a couple of times. Nothing happens. He turns on the light on his cell and uses it to illuminate a dark corridor. Broken glass and pebbles crunch under our feet. We pass empty offices with desks covered in thick layers of dust. In parts, the ceiling has given way. Broken beams touch the floor and let thin slivers of light inside.

I spot a stack of books on a shelf. As I touch it, it collapses into a heap of dust. I jump back and cough.

"Over here," my partner says. He holds up a book with a thick leather cover. "This must be a journal."

Some pages in the middle are stuck together, but we manage to pry it open with careful fingers. Several of the first pages crumble to dust as we do, but the last half of the book remains intact.

"What *is* this?" The handwritten scribbles inside are in an unfamiliar language.

"Hang on." He scans the page with his cell and stares at the screen. "It's Greek." I stare at him while he reads silently. His face turns as ashen as the dust around us, then he flips the page and scans again.

"Come on, you—"

"Shh!" He repeats the process a few times while I study our surroundings. My eyes have adjusted to the dark by now. I spot faded icons of forgotten saints on the crumbly walls. They glare at us from the shadows, as if we're violating the sanctity of the place. Their faces creep me out, so I lift my gaze to examine the sickly sky through a hole in the ceiling.

He reads the last page and raises defeated eyes at me. "I think I know what happened," he says. He sounds as if he's choking on gravel.

My heart skips a beat. "Yes?"

He draws a deep breath. "After we killed Hitler, Germany basically imploded. Two months later, Stalin invaded. After occupying Germany, he attacked Poland. Then, the Allies declared war on Russia." He takes my hand. "There never was a Cold War. Just a decades-long hot one. The States got the bomb first, but the Russians did so just a month later. The second part of the war was fought with nukes."

I stare at him in disbelief. Numbness spreads from my head to my toes. My lips move before I can think. "If this place was nuked, how did any of this survive?"

"It wasn't hit directly. This"—he motions around us—"is the result of the fallout. The nuclear winter has lasted well over a century. The monk who wrote this describes how all of his brothers died of radiation poisoning." His face drops as his gaze scans the condemning faces on the walls. "His last entry was over a hundred years ago. We may well be the last people alive." He gives me a resigned half shrug. "Not for long, of course. Radiation is probably killing us as we speak."

Despite myself, I burst into a cracked cackle.

"What's wrong with you?" he asks, a flash of anger in his voice.

"We broke history." My head spins. *Is radiation already killing me?* My legs buckle and my knees hit the ground, raising a cloud of ash. Burning tears streak down my cheeks. "We broke history."

He kneels next to me and takes me in his arms. I gasp as our surroundings fade around us. This time, they disappear into a blinding flash of light.

"Hold still," a woman's voice says.

Hands pull at my face. I slap them away, then my eyes focus on a woman's face a few inches away. A woman in a blue beret is pulling away virtual reality goggles.

"The dizziness will soon pass," she says in a professional voice. "You should lie still until then."

I nod and nausea hits me. I shut my eyes. "Where am I?"

She pulls a needle leading to a transparent tube from my arm, making me cringe. "Back at the training camp. Your memories will return shortly."

I absentmindedly rub a red spot on my arm, where the needle used to be. It stings. She removes spider-like electrodes from my temples and memories rush into my head as if a floodgate has ripped open. The experience from the time travel fades away, leaving an acrid taste in my mouth, like waking up from a nightmare. I haven't time-traveled yet. Today was part of the training. A warning to the dangers of messing with the timeline.

"I *told* you it was too easy," a groggy voice says. On a bed next to mine, my partner is grinning at me, ignoring a male nurse who is flicking a penlight at his eyes.

"Hey, you," I say. My voice is hoarse, as if my throat has been sandblasted.

The woman and the nurse move in front of a large monitor displaying various readings and exchange notes in low voices. Every now and then they glance at us and tap on a tablet.

I turn my attention back to my partner. I've had my eye on him for a while now. I remember my excitement at getting him as my exercise partner. "Hell of a first date," I say, a dry smile on my lips.

"At least we got to kiss."

My cheeks feel hot.

"But you're right. Let me make it up to you," he continues with a wide grin and a mischievous sparkle in his warm hazel eyes. "Dinner at Freddo's?"

I check out his handsome face and broad shoulders. Even lying on that bed, his wide frame is imposing. My heart flutters as I mimic his grin. "Sure, why not. Meet you at eight?"

The grin on his face widens as his head slumps back on his pillow. "Deal."

Shh—the Baby's Sleeping

The Patient

"He's awake."

I stir in my sleep, lost in unsettling dreams. There's a fire. Ashes. Acrid smoke burning my throat. I moan, only half-awake. "Hmm?"

He nudges me again. "Come on, honey," he says with a pleading voice. "It's your turn. I went last time."

My eyes flutter open. *Thank goodness, it was just a dream.* I rub cobwebs from my eyelids, then shut them again with a throaty groan. "Just five more minutes, then I'll go. Promise." I'm almost asleep again when our son's wailing echoes in the room. I push the soft, warm duvet away and swivel my legs off the bed. "Shush, darling. Mommy's coming."

As my feet touch the cold floor, I steal a look at my husband, his mouth half-open, his eyes completely shut. I can hear light snoring in the brief spaces between the baby's hungry yelps. I fight the urge to throw a pillow at him as I stumble out of bed and toward the crib in the corner. I don't turn on the lamp, using instead the little sliver of light slipping from under the door and between the window curtains to guide myself through the all-too-familiar room.

"*Shh, shh.* I'm here, darling," I say and stroke the baby's face. The crying stops as his hungry lips root for my finger. He opens big blue eyes, his dad's eyes, to stare at me. The eyelids are red with sleep, and I gently wipe a tear away from one of them. He grabs my hand and squeezes with all his might. Even in my sleep, my heart melts. Angel hair surrounds his lovely face. Cherry, half-open lips open hungrily. A knitted beige bear smiles at me from his chest.

I kiss his stubby little fingers and wait for him to release me, then head over to the fridge and fetch a milk bottle. My hand reaches for the microwave door. For a second, it pauses before the door as a fleeting memory of a fire tries to emerge into my head. It evaporates as soon as it reaches the surface of my consciousness. *Stupid dream.* With a shudder, I open the microwave door and hit the button that will warm up the milk for exactly one minute.

While drowsy seconds count down to zero, my gaze caresses my baby. He looks so peaceful, so beautiful. *God, I love them both so much. If anything should happen to them, I'd probably lose my mind.*

The beep from the microwave snaps me out of my reverie, and I open the microwave door.

The Doctor

My hand reaches for the switch and turns off the monitor. "Now you've seen her," I tell the beautiful young woman.

She leans back into her chair. "She does this every day?"

"*She* has a name. Jane." The words coming out of my mouth sound like cracked ice. I didn't mean them to, but I can see in her eyes nothing but pity for Jane. And I hate that. Jane's to be helped; taken care of—not pitied.

She raises her hands before her in an apologetic manner. "I'm sorry. So, *Jane* does this every day?"

"Yes. She replays the last twenty-four hours with them. When she reaches the point of the fire, it's like her brain reboots and it starts all over again."

She shakes her head in amazement. "Her scars are the result of the fire?"

"You mean her face?"

She tilts her head in question. "There are more?"

"The scars actually go all the way down her body, but I guess the robe hides that." I reach for a folder on my desk and pull out a bunch of photos. When I pass them to the woman, she flinches. To her credit, she studies them, one after the other, before handing them back to me. Only the pallor on her face betrays they had any effect on her. *She's tough, I'll give her that.* "When she came to us, it was touch and go," I say as I slip the photos back into the folder. "But we have a great trauma specialist—one of the best in the country. I'm not worried about her body. It's the scars in her soul that worry me the most."

"I can see that." She taps her finger against shapely lips. "I noticed there's no mirror in the room."

My shoulders lift in a half shrug. "With or without one, she spends half an hour each day staring at the wall where the bedroom mirror used to sit, combing non-existent hair with a plastic fork she believes is a comb."

Her eyes light up and she nods. "She only sees what she wants to," she says, finally understanding.

"Exactly. She is no more likely to notice her scars than she is to realize that she's feeding a plastic doll, or that her husband is a pillow." I steeple my fingers before me. "Which is why I can't let you proceed with the treatment."

Her eyes widen. "Excuse me?"

"You want to cure her. What good would come out of it? This way, she's happy. She's whole. She's well taken care of. She lacks for nothing." I lean forward, planting my elbows on my desk. "Imagine you wake up from the best dream you've ever had, and face a nightmare of a reality. In your dream, you are loved. Safe. In reality, you're alone. Scared. You've lost everyone and everything you've ever loved. Would you want that?"

She straightens her back. "I can see your point but, with all due respect, that's not your decision."

"I'm afraid I have to insist. As her attending doctor—"

She interrupts me with a slightly raised voice. "Both the trustees and her sister—"

"Can go to hell," I burst out and bang my fist on the desk. She gapes at me, eyes as big as teacups. I run my hand through my hair. "I apologize. It's just..." I force myself to draw a deep breath before I continue. "It's just that I feel very strongly about this."

"I understand." Her tone is ice-cold.

"No, you don't." I rub my temples to ease the sudden thumping in my head. "I knew them. Knew her. We were friends before she even met her husband. Before they got married, started a family. I gave her my word all those years ago. To look after her, no matter what. And this treatment is not in her best interest."

"Not your decision," she repeats. She speaks the words simply, matter-of-factly. "She's broken now, but we can restore her. Make her whole again."

"She's not a broken toy to be fixed, for God's sake. She's a human being." I can see my words have no effect on her. My cheeks heat up.

"We can bring back her memories," she continues, as if she hasn't heard me. "Within a month, this pointless existence can end. Her sister has gone to great lengths to ensure that Jane has access to the treatment."

I clench my jaw at the mention of the old hag. She never cared for Jane before. And now, she doesn't care how much pain her sudden interest in her sister's so-called well-being will bring. "Why?" The word leaves my lips before I can think.

She shrugs. "She's my boss, not my friend. I'm only here to let you know we'll be transferring her out next week." She jumps to her feet to indicate this was just a courtesy call. One that is now over.

Her short skirt does nothing to hide long, shapely legs as she leans forward, hand extended. She looks like a skinny insect. One I want to swat.

"Thank you for everything you've done for her," she says. "We'll be in touch to arrange the transfer."

I cross my arms before my chest and meet her gaze in defiance. As she eventually lowers her hand, she knocks the lamp over. She rushes to put it upright again.

You clumsy idiot. "Please," I beg through gritted teeth. "To you, she's a deformed monster. A problem to be fixed. To me, she's a very dear friend. One I've cared about for a long time. As I said, I've made a promise. And I won't break it."

"I'm sorry. The decision's been made." She spins around and marches toward the door.

"Miss!" I call out just as she reaches for the handle. "I'll need your boss's current details. I'm afraid I've lost touch with her, and I'd like to talk to her myself. Explain the situation."

She pauses for a moment, her fingers already wrapped around the silver handle. Without turning, she speaks a number.

I hurriedly grab a pen and a piece of paper and jot it down. "Her address, too."

She turns sideways and chews her lip, then gives me that as well.

"Thank you." I wave dismissively, and she shuts the door on her way out. Louder than she has to, but I don't care.

I pour myself a large one. To my dismay, my hand shakes, rattling the ice cubes. I down it in one large gulp, then pour a second one. My mind is racing, exploring options. I could sue. Go to court. But I'm not a relative. Her sister would win. Plus, if the trustees are behind this ridiculous decision, I could even lose my job.

I groan and slam the glass on the table, almost knocking over the lamp. I hate feeling cornered. Helpless. I stare at the diplomas on the wall with unseeing eyes as my fingers rap against the desk's hard wood. That annoying young insect is right. They *will* take her from me, and there's nothing I can do. *Unless...*

I slump backwards and the back of my head hits the leather chair. I reach for the glass and take a slow sip. There is but one option. The *only* option. Terrible as it might be, I can't think of a better way.

I reach into my pocket and pull out a key. One I haven't used in years. I run my fingers over the dull metal, feeling the grooves and indentations, as memories flood my head. Then, my hand hovers over the bottom drawer. The one that's been locked for years. As if they have a mind of their own, my fingers slide the key into the lock and turn twice. The drawer clicks softly.

I hesitate. My mind is frantically looking for another option, but there is none. I know that meddling sister well. As stubborn a person as they come. Haven't seen her in years, but I'm sure that old age will have only made her worse. She'd never see reason. *Make her whole.* I scoff. She *is* whole. She has her family to take care of. Me, to take care of her. What more can she ever need?

But her sister doesn't see it that way. She'll never understand that she'll be condemning Jane to a lifetime of despair. That's why I stopped her from seeing Jane in the first place. She was always asking awkward questions, always prying. Always making Jane relive that awful experience. Doesn't she care at all for her sister's happiness? *What am I talking about? That selfish bitch never cared about Jane. Always turning me away, when all I ever wanted was to make Jane happy.* No, there is no other way. I have to pay the woman a visit.

I jerk the drawer open. I'd almost lost Jane twice. Once, when she got married. And then, when the detonator had misfired, almost killing her in the fire. I can't bear the thought of losing her again. Not after everything we've been through.

From inside the open drawer, a detonator stares at me, its silver surface bright and shiny as if barely a day had passed since I last used its twin. I pick it up and gently stroke the smooth surface. *It's time for another fire.*

The Sister

I press rewind. The footage that my agent has secured is grainy, and the angle from the top of the table lamp is not great. It's good enough to confirm my suspicions, though. I've never liked the man. That mousy doctor, who used to hound my sister even as a nerdy kid. I'd fought him when he wanted to look after her, but I'd lost. He was the expert, and I was just the paranoid sister.

We'll see who's paranoid now. I was *sure* he'd refuse her the treatment she needed. He's already cut me off; prevented me from seeing her all these years. But taking her away from his greedy little hands wasn't enough. Not for me. Not for her. Not for her family.

I freeze the scene and zoom in. Inside the drawer, I can clearly see a detonator-like device. I have to check my records, but it looks identical to the one found in my sister's bedroom ashes. And when we treat her and she regains her memories, I know what she'll tell us she saw the night of the fire. *Whom* she saw.

A wide grin crawls on my face. I hit a button on the phone sitting on my desk. A moment later, a woman's voice answers. "Police. How may I help you?"

I clear my throat. "I need to speak to one of your detectives. I have some fresh information about a cold case."

You're in for a Ride: Part II

I have no idea how much time has passed, my sleep uneasy with these strange dreams. A man opens the door, waking me up rudely. Long shadows cover his face. A suede fedora covers the top of his head, thick raindrops dripping along its edge. A long, beige trench coat, straight out of a last century movie, completes the unusual outfit. He leaves wide wet stains on the seat and floor. It's the eyes that grab my attention, though. Straight out of hell. Yellow, with an orange flame dancing within. Demonic.

I shudder and fight the instinct to flee. "Where to, mister?"

He gives me an address at the city's derelict warehouse area. His voice, a snake crawling over gravel. It sends the small hairs on my back to stand up in attention. I swallow to wet my dry throat, then punch in the address. As the cab gently swerves into the street and takes off, I keep stealing glances in the mirror. The flames in the man's eyes grow with each passing moment. The storm outside is picking up. I can feel its chill in my bones and turn up the heating. When lightning flashes, I practically jump out of my skin.

The ride feels endless. I almost let out a sigh of relief when we pull over. Derelict buildings litter the unlit street. We stop before a rundown colonial house, strangely out of place among the shattered-windowed warehouses and abandoned tenement halls. It might have been pretty a couple of centuries ago, but has turned into a creepy shell of its former self by now.

"Wait here." He lifts his collar and steps out in the stormy night, ignoring the gusts of wind that whip him with dark water.

I stare at the empty cabin for a moment, savoring his absence. Then, my bowels growl and a rumbling, sharp pain instructs me to look for the closest toilet. That's one thing they still haven't been able to fit into a modern-day cab, and I curse silently its designers.

A neon light flashes in the distance. I can't make it out, but it has to be a bar, or an all-day convenience store. I chew my lip for a while, then a second pang in my guts makes me jump out of the cab and hurry down the street.

Icy raindrops whip my face like tiny darts. My feet splash in freezing puddles. A TV is drowning the wailing of a baby, while a couple's shouts—its parents?—assault me as I rush down the street. As I approach, I can see the name of the place: *The Phantom*. My mouth twitches, but my legs keep walking toward the entrance. The windows are too misted to see inside, but lit. I can hear people chattering and glasses clinking. After a moment's hesitation, my hand reaches for the handle. As soon as I touch it, it disintegrates into a pile of rust, swept away by a sudden gust of bitter wind.

All sounds cease. No tipsy patrons, no laughter, no drunken toasts. No crying babies, no fighting couples, no TV. The windows are as dark as the rest of the street. I almost empty my bowels right there and then. Instead, I whirl around and hurry back to the safety of the cab. *Screw this, I'm out of here.*

Behind me, I hear footsteps. Without turning my head, I know who it is. I shove my hands into my pockets and walk faster. Instead of closing the distance, the cab looks farther away. Soon, I am panting, walking turning into running. My heart is pounding against my chest. Yet, I can hear the footsteps closing in.

I make a sharp left into the colonial house, hoping to shake him off. Darkness covers the entrance. Cobwebs jiggle in the wind. I push them aside and bolt down a derelict stairway. I have to escape his foul presence.

The stairway ends on a metal door. Rusted hinges keep it closed. A naked lamp illuminates the cramped space, its pale yellow light struggling to exorcise the surrounding black.

His footsteps echo behind me, closer and closer. I take a step back and throw myself at the door with all my might. It groans but refuses to budge. My shoulder burns.

I ignore it and shove the metal once again. And again. His footsteps are almost upon me when the door finally gives way and I lose my balance. I tumble down half a dozen steps and land on all fours on muddy soil. In what little light creeps into the room from the busted door, I make out bodies lying all around me. I touch one, and it crumbles under my trembling fingers. *Mummified.* The word rings in my head, drowning out all thought.

I lift my head to see the man's silhouette against the open frame. An all-consuming fire is now twirling in his eyes. I scurry backwards, but before I can blink he's upon me. He grabs my head with his hands. Spiked tendrils shoot out from his palms, digging into my flesh. I struggle to free myself but am unable to move. He licks his lips, parting them into a hungry smile. Fiery pain fills my head. I open my mouth to scream, but no sound comes out. After an eternity of agony, he pushes his thumb into my mouth and something shoots into my stomach. A seed.

An overpowering weakness consumes me. I close my eyes and welcome the darkness that swallows me.

***

I wake up with a jolt. I'm back in my cab, waiting at the train station. *Damn you, woman, and your professor.* I rub the sleep out of my eyes. Despite the cold, I'm covered in thick beads of sweat. I debate taking a few steps outside, but it's still pouring. I press a button and the misted window rolls down. Raindrops whip my face, my hands, my legs. They land on the dashboard and smudge the displays. With a muffled curse, I roll the window back up.

My breathing has barely returned to normal when the last train pulls in. A moment later, it spits out drowsy passengers. They march out in long lines before vanishing into the darkness, unsteady steps turning into hurried ones.

A man opens the door and steps into the cab. Long shadows cover his face. A suede fedora covers the top of his head, thick raindrops dripping along its edge. A long, beige trench coat, straight out of a last century movie, completes the unusual outfit. It leaves wide wet stains on the seat and floor. It's the eyes that grab my attention, though. I swear, they're yellow, with an orange flame dancing within.

My eyes widen in recognition. I struggle to keep my voice calm. "Where to?"

He gives me an address and my blood turns to ice. The address is at the city's derelict warehouse area.

As the cab gently swerves into the street and takes off, I keep stealing glances in the mirror. The flames in the man's eyes grow with each passing moment. The storm outside is picking up. I can feel its chill in my bones and turn up the heating. When lightning flashes, I practically jump out of my skin.

The ride feels endless. I almost let out a sigh of relief when we pull over. Derelict buildings litter the unlit street. We stop before a familiar colonial house that's seen better days.

"Wait here." He lifts his collar and steps out in the stormy night, ignoring the gusts of wind that whip him with dark water.

He disappears into the house, confirming my worst fears. I fidget on my seat. My fingers drum against the dashboard. My foot taps the floor. Then, I can't wait any longer. I must stop him, if it's the last thing I do.

I burst out of the cab and follow him inside. I push cobwebs out of my face as I step through the dark entrance. I hurry down the stairs. A naked lamp illuminates a broken door, hanging from rusted hinges.

My hands can't stop shaking as I step through the gaping opening and stagger down half a dozen creaking steps. Bodies litter the muddy floor. Only the *drip drip drip* of rain can be heard.

The man is slumping over one of the corpses. He spins around to face me, his eyes burning with excitement. "I've found it," he says, his voice cracking the gloomy silence.

"What is this place?" I ask as I take a careful step toward him, making sure to stay between him and the door.

"It's the Phantom's lair. The final piece of proof. They thought me crazy. Now I'll show them. We can finally rid the world of this creature." He motions around. "There are at least two dozen bodies in here. We should call the cops."

My eyes widen in surprise. "You're the professor." I hesitate for a moment, then take another step. It brings me almost next to him. He leans to the ground and pulls at a hand sticking out of the mud. It detaches from the arm and he lands on his back, splashing muddy waters everywhere. "Give me a hand, will you?" he groans as he tries to free himself from the soil. His gaze jumps to the severed limb and he chuckles. "A hand, get it?"

I have to be more careful. Had my dream not warned me about him, I would have been doomed. The thought is echoing in my head as I hurry by his side and grab his head. Spiked tendrils shoot out from my palms, digging into his flesh. He struggles to free himself, but the poison works fast and he's unable to move. I lick my lips, parting them into a hungry smile. With him, I have enough bodies for my babies. He opens his mouth to scream, but no sound comes out. I collect his life force at my fingertip and fill a seed with it, then shove my thumb into the open orifice. The now pregnant seed shoots from under my fingernail and into his body. Within a few decades, it will grow into a healthy baby.

A moment later, he closes his eyes and his body turns limp in my hands.

Still buzzing with the remainders of his life force cruising through my veins, I gently lay his dead body down on the ground and watch the mud open up to swallow him. "Don't worry. You're the last one—for now." I stay on all fours for a while, waiting for the room to stop spinning. My eyes turn to the still body. "Besides, you'll rise again. After all, even gods need someone to worship them."

Bonus Stories

If you enjoyed these stories, please keep reading for some further stories from my collections, *The Power of Six Infinite Waters*, and *Honest Fibs*, available on Amazon.

What's in a Name?

"That's an unusual name for a ship."

The man facing me across the table pulled the fat cigar from his lips, leaving it to simmer inside a round ashtray. Smoking is strictly prohibited on a spaceship, but if you are the ship's owner I guess normal rules do not apply. His thick brows met in the middle, as if pondering my words. Why, I could not fathom — surely, this was the single most usual comment he heard? His jowls quivered as he pushed his chair away to stand up. Hoisting his trousers up, he adjusted his lifejacket and grimaced, as if in pain.

"It was a bet." With a dismissive wave of his hand, he motioned me to follow him. "A stupid bet." He sighed as he ran his fingers through thinning hair. "I lost."

That much is obvious. "Are we going somewhere?" I asked politely and stood up. My recorder floated from the table to hover above us.

"I just want to show you around. I assume your viewers will want to know about the ship?"

I nodded my thanks. We weaved our way out of the smoke room and into the promenade deck. Reserved for the first-class passengers, this was not my usual kind of accommodation. My initial enthusiasm at finding out I had been sent on an assignment that allowed me to spend a week on a cruise around the moon had waned as soon as I heard the details. The lush accommodations, however, made me rethink my initial apprehension.

The ship owner led me into the wide corridor crossing the deck. I snuck a look into a gym room, filled with ripped people in sweatpants admiring their visage in full-wall mirrors. Strangely enough, the lifejackets did not seem to bother them. A smiling blonde at the reception was handing a towel and a lifejacket to a man dressed from top to bottom in grey flannel. Splashing was heard from a wide, steel-framed door behind her. I guessed the sounds came from an indoor swimming pool. Judging by the steam on the glass, the doors next to it led to a spa or sauna. My muscles ached for a massage, but that would have to wait. I was here for a job.

"Do they wear lifejackets in the pool?" I wondered aloud. I guessed that an inflatable nanosuit that could keep you alive for an hour in space would probably be waterproof, but it still seemed strange.

"Everyone has to wear their lifejacket twenty-four-seven. It's part of the insurance policy." For the first time since we met, the foreboding cloud lifted from his eyes and the man grinned. "It gives them something to tell their friends after the cruise."

"Is the name also why you only do moon cruises, instead of Mars ones? To avoid any stray comets?"

"Can't be too careful," the man agreed.

I stepped aside as a slender girl rushed out a door and almost crashed on us. She was balancing half a dozen e-books and tablets, taken from what I guessed was the lending library. With a shy smile, she dashed down the corridor and into the reading room. Her lifejacket bounced against the doorframe, almost making her drop the devices, but she managed to hold on to them at the last moment.

"Are you coming?"

Despite his short stature and rotund figure, the ship owner could move fast. I hurried up after him, my eye catching on the Renaissance-style trimmings. The decoration was worthy of a floating five-star hotel. All first-class common rooms were adorned with ornate wood paneling and expensive furniture instead of the practical simplicity usually found on spaceships.

We passed an open door leading to the outside deck. In a few hours, this would be filled with a throng of passengers socializing, promenading or relaxing in hired deck chairs and sculpted wooden benches. An artificial sun would be shining on the dome covering the ship. Now, however, the deck lay empty, much like the space surrounding us. I stole a look outside. The vast emptiness of space caught my breath. Countless stars sparkled brighter than anything I had ever seen back on Earth. Our movement was so smooth, that it felt like sailing on a quiet pond. I half-expected a flock of wild geese to land on the deck at any moment.

Someone closed the door and passed me by, snapping me back to the present. I followed the ship owner down the Grand Staircase, one of the most distinctive features of the ship. It descended through seven decks. A dome of wrought iron and glass would welcome the artificial sunlight in the morning, although it now lay dark, like a black, polished diamond. A large, carved wooden panel above us contained a clock, with figures of "Honour and Glory crowning Time" flanking the clock face. I could not help but gape at the beauty of it all.

Upon reaching the landing, we entered an ornate hall lit by gold-plated light fixtures. Well-laid tables filled the room. White linen covered the tops. Silver cutlery clanked against porcelain dishes. Waiters meandered skillfully to serve dinner to hungry first-class passengers.

Music came from the far end, drowning out the diners' soft murmur. I recognized "O mio Babbino Caro" and half-expected to hear a soprano—maybe even Callas herself, brought back from the dead—singing the aria. "The Café Parisien offers the best French haute cuisine for first-class passengers," the man said with a well-practiced flourish.

"And the music?"

"Our very own small *ensemble*. Eight musicians, the very best."

"They'd have to be, to play with their lifejackets on," I could not help but joke.

He did not seem to share my mirth, and muttered something under his breath. He spun around to continue the tour, when a jolt reverberated through the hull. It was so strong that it knocked me off my feet, sending me to land on my lifejacket. A mannequin crashed through a glass display and dropped next to me. *I survived a cruise on…* , the t-shirt it wore read. The rest of the inscription was obscured by the doll's broken arm.

I heard shouts all around me. Angry claxons blared in alarm. People clamored. Lights dimmed, and shone again. Then, it all stopped. An eerie silence fell. Dazed people struggled to get their bearings. Expensive leather shoes and elegant high heels stepped on salmon and pheasant as stunned diners rose to their feet. Fear and silent pleas for help filled the passengers' eyes. I turned to the ship owner, but he had disappeared. From afar, I heard one long continuous wailing hiss, like locusts on a midsummer night in the woods. *Are we decompressing?* I decided to follow the noise. The flickering lights allowed me to reach the nearest exit, pushing through the nervous throng.

I had just reached the door handle when the floor tilted. The vessel reared up, followed by a rumbling roar and a muffled explosion. I pushed through the door and grabbed the railing. Above me, the dome cracked. A small chunk flew away, blown out by the pressure. My eyes gaped at the ugly sight. A second piece followed. The ship let out a terrible groan and quivered, like a mongrel trying to throw the fleas off its back. *Crack!* The dome split open with a deafening blast. Deck chairs and sculpted wooden benches flew around me to burst through the fracture. The clamor drowned out my scream.

The gushing atmosphere sucked me upwards. The shock took the breath out of my lungs. I flew towards the dome at an increasing speed, gasping for air. The lifejacket sprang to life. Nanocarbon blades clasped and banded together to form an impenetrable barrier that covered me from head to toe. Air hissed in my ears. After a heart-stopping moment of weightlessness, I crashed against the dome and yelled in pain. My hands grabbed the dome's torn edge. I held on for a moment, my feet already dangling in space. I started sliding, carried away by the rushing air. My eyes searched in vain for anything to hold on to. Then, I let go.

I popped through the gap in the dome, like a cork. I drifted away from the safety of the spaceship and into the endless void of space. I flailed my arms and legs to stop the dizzying motion. My heart beat so fast, I thought it would pop out of my chest. Finally, it occurred to me to let my lifejacket guide me to safety. Valves hissed and the mad rotation stopped, just as I was about to hurl my stomach's contents against my mask.

Something banged against me. I spun around, startled, and came up against a lifeboat. An airlock opened up silently before me. Too exhausted to haul myself, I let the men already inside pull me in.

The door behind me closed in silence. Air hissed into the airlock. My ears popped as sound returned. I punched the clasp deactivating the lifejacket. With a soft clicking sound, it retracted back into my belt, ready to spring back to life at a moment's notice. I landed on the metal floor, still nauseated. It smelled of engine oil, petrol and ozone. The sweetest smell to ever hit my nostrils. Someone helped me to my feet and sat me down. I nodded my thanks and coughed to clear my lungs. Tears burned my eyes and my throat.

"Are you all right?"

Recognizing the voice, I looked up and saw the ship owner. "I will be, thanks," I rasped after a moment. I drew a deep breath, grateful to be alive. "What the hell happened?"

"A ship collided with us," the man said. "Those idiots must have been drunk or something."

I shook my head. I had heard stories of crews drinking on the job, but this was one for the books. The huge cruise ship was not exactly hard to miss.

I glanced outside. The dome had now disappeared.

Silent explosions dotted the ship's hull. Numerous lifeboats shot out of gaping holes in the decks. A second spaceship tilted drunkenly next to it. In the darkness of space, it was hard to make out, but it looked like a freighter.

My eye caught on something like countless heads bobbing around is. "My God," I whispered. "Are those people?"

The man leaned next to me and craned his head to look. "No, that's not heads." He looked forlorn. "It's lettuce. Frozen lettuce. That damn ship was filled with it. Probably for the moon colonies." His eyes glinted with something akin to madness. "We were struck by a freighter carrying iceberg lettuce."

"Iceberg lett—" I coughed to swallow the mad cackle that rose to my throat, shaking my head. "Buddy, *that's* why you don't call your ship the Titanic II."

Little Star Corvette

"You don't mind if we meet at Sirrah, do you, hon?" Kate asked. "I can be there in a couple of days."

"Aw, come on. You know I hate driving alone."

"Something's come up."

I keep my voice calm. "You promised to meet me at the Andromeda Junction. Said you couldn't wait."

She stifled one of her signature yawns. The ones that signified she no longer cared for our conversation. I'd got enough of those when we broke up to recognize them anywhere. "Sorry."

I knew I'd already lost the argument. I tapped my glasses to close the connection. Punched them, more like it. If she asked—which she wouldn't—I'd just say the connection got cut off. Always a risk with subspace communication, after all. Not that she'd believe me. She knew me too well for that.

Having a Star Corvette Mark Nine and no one to share it with was no fun. When the company handed her over for a test drive, I thought I'd be picking up a different babe on each space station. But the unholy schedule they gave me meant there were no hot women when I arrived to each of my destinations; just unshaven, half-asleep groups of mechanics with soiled uniforms and grease under their nails.

"Great," I mumbled. Now even Kate, my failsafe ex, had bailed on me. Supposedly to meet her girlfriends, but I knew the truth: She hated waking up before noon. She was probably already asleep by the time I cut off the connection.

I shoved my hands into my pockets and paced in front of the slender, eight-foot-long ship hovering above the extended arm of the space dock. She was the prettiest thing I'd ever driven, all nimble and sexy, with the new warp drive purring softly in her underbelly and a ride so smooth it could be a limo. No other ship around matched her elegant beauty—not that there were many at this hour. What's the point of all that, though, with no one gawking at me in jealousy? I'd already been flying this baby all around the galaxy for a week now, and had nothing to show for it save two speeding tickets. Even worse, this was the last day before I had to take her back. She wouldn't hit the market for another six months, which meant I wouldn't be able to lay my hands on another one of these beauties for at least that long. Not that I could ever afford one, of course.

I kicked its smooth red surface. Not too hard, just to vent off. As expected, the coating, specially designed for both subspace and normal space, bent under my foot, then sprang back to its original shape.

"That will show it," a nasal, professorial voice behind me said.

I whirled around to find a short, balding man in worn tweed staring with admiration at the ship. *Not only does he sound like a professor, he looks like one, too.* Instead of the augmented reality eyewear everyone wore, a pair of plain plastic spectacles covered his beady eyes. *Is that tape holding the bridge together?* My gaze scanned his clothes. Even the suede elbow patches matched the voice. His jacket sagged, as if he had been caught in a shrinking ray and now all his clothes were two sizes too large. I chuckled. *That would explain how thin he is.*

He scratched the threadlike stubble on his chin and pointed politely at the Corvette. "Nice ship."

"Thanks."

"A prototype, is it?"

A proud grin parted my lips, which was silly. The ship wasn't mine. I was just one of many test drivers, barely making minimum wage. Still, there it was: someone was finally ogling her. I grinned like a child licking the only ice cream in the neighborhood, all of his friends watching with envy. "Yep. Mark Nine, and .07 warp. Could take you to Alpheratz and back in six hours."

The man let out a slow whistle. "I've read about them. Thought they weren't due this year."

I shrugged. "They aren't. I'm test driving this one."

He licked his lips. "I've never been on a Star Corvette. Wonder if you'd like some company?"

"I don't…" I trailed off. Why the hell not? Kate had just blown me off. And I had to go to Sirrah anyway. He was hardly the hot blonde I was hoping for, but at least I wouldn't be alone. "I'm headed to Sirrah," I said with a resigned sigh.

"I thought you said Alpheratz?"

"Figure of speech. No, I have to return this to the Sirrah space station by tomorrow."

"That's perfect. Been meaning to visit some friends there." He gave me a pleading look. "So?"

My lips twitched upwards. "Fine. Hop aboard."

To my surprise, he did just that. No luggage, no nothing. He literally hopped into the airlock and reappeared a second later inside the cockpit. He thumped the thick glass that framed it. "Are you coming?" he mouthed, and pointed to the driver's seat.

With a shrug, I ambled inside and sank into the velvet softness of my seat with a contented sigh.

He was gawking at the leather-like material, running his fingers up and down the armrest. "That's some sweet fabric," he said, marvel in his voice. "Smooth like a baby's bottom."

The last baby's bottom I'd seen was my own, so I just shrugged and started the preflight sequence. "It's okay," I said, trying to sound nonchalant.

His eyes bulged behind those thick lenses. "Just okay? It's awesome, man!" With his finger, he pressed his glasses up his nose, as if his bulging eyes had pushed them away.

I chuckled, the contrast between his clothes and demeanor amusing me. "Yeah, all right," I said and ran a finger along the seat's rim. "It's pretty sweet."

He rapped his fingers against the glass and bounced up and down on his seat, like an eager five-year-old with a full bladder. I ignored him while I finished the preflight checklist and navigated away from the Andromeda Junction.

Once we were away from the station, he jumped on his seat to face me again. "So, what's next?"

"Sirrah." I keyed in the coordinates and the subspace drive hummed to life. I held on to my armrests. No matter how many times I'd done this, it still felt wrong. Like punching a hole into the fabric of time and space, just because humanity couldn't wait to move from point A to point B fast enough. The glass around us darkened for a split second, then a light like a thousand suns exploding blinded us. Every molecule in my body did a little jiggle as we slipped into subspace. Then, everything went dark again.

I checked the instruments. A rapidly accelerating number shone on the monitor. Within ten seconds, it steadied. We were traveling at one fifth the speed of light. "Point oh two," I said with unwarranted pride.

He let out a whistle. "Damn, that's impressive. I hardly felt it."

"It's the new inertia dampers. They're twice as smooth as anything before them."

"That is so cool." He pointed at the speed, a cheeky grin on his face. "Is that the fastest she can go?"

I scrunched up my nose as I instinctively checked the monitor. The number two blinked leisurely in a glowing red. "I've already got two citations on this trip. Another one and I lose my license."

"Sorry to hear that. Speeding?"

I clicked my tongue. "Stupid cops. Subspace is vast. I don't understand why they even need to monitor traffic here. You have fewer chances of running into another ship than lightning striking you in the middle of a zombie apocalypse as you win the lottery."

He laughed; a hearty, genuine chortle. "Politicians. They have to pass laws to make themselves useful. Even if they make no sense."

Nodding my agreement, I made sure all systems were a go before leaning back in my chair. "So, what did you say you do?"

He pursed his lips for a moment, as if considering his answer. "I'm a techsmith."

"A what?"

"A techsmith," he repeated with conviction.

My brow furrowed. "Never heard of it. What's that?"

He did a little twirl with his thumbs as he stared into the glass ceiling. "What do you call someone who has a way with words?"

"A writer?"

He shook his head in disappointment. "A wordsmith. And someone who's good at unlocking stuff?"

Ah. I was beginning to see where this was going. "A locksmith?"

"Now you're getting it."

"So, you're good with tech stuff. A hacker, then."

He drew a sharp breath through closed lips, as if I had insulted him, and clicked his tongue. "That's like comparing a goldsmith to a toddler making pottery."

I laughed. "Well, Mr. Techsmith, I'm not sure what you want me to say. Even if you're the world's best hacker, it wouldn't do you much good in here. This ship is impervious to any sort of cyberattack."

His face clouded. He glared at me through lowered spectacles, then absent-mindedly played with the frame of his glasses as he stared out of the window. Of course, the only thing he could see in subspace was the faint illumination of the iridescent bubble surrounding our ship. His sudden interest in the void could only mean I had offended him.

Great. Me and my big mouth. I let out a mental sigh and braced myself for a few silent hours, when a display turned red.

"Preparing for emergency exit from subspace," the computer's voice said in a casual tone that belied the threat behind its words. "Exiting subspace in ten..." Numbers counted down on my monitor, flickering to attract my attention, as if the ominous countdown were not enough.

"What the…" I punched keys and pushed levers, but nothing changed.

"Two… one…"

Flash! The darkness of normal space popped into existence. I blinked to clear my vision. Billions of stars glinted around us.

"Why…" I checked the controls. Everything looked normal again. "Did you…"

He gave me a satisfied grin, like a cat that had just burped a single yellow feather.

"But how? You didn't even…"

He gave me a small shrug. "Told you. I'm a techsmith."

It was my turn to let out a slow whistle. "Bloody hell. You really are. Say, can you—"

Out of the corner of my eye I caught a bright flash. Red and blue lights lit up our cockpit, followed by a burst of static in our speakers. "This is Officer Smith," a soft voice said. "Good morning, gentlemen. Where's the fire?"

Crap! The cops. I opened a channel. "Erm, what fire, Officer?"

"So, you performed an emergency subspace exit without something being on fire?" The voice could have been described as gentle; joyful even. Somehow, that made a drop of sweat appear on my forehead.

"It was a malfunction, Officer. Nothing I could do about it." The drop of sweat trickled down my temple. I shot my passenger a furious glare as I wiped it away. "Help me," I mouthed. An expression of deep remorse failed to appear on his face. I probably would have strangled him right then and there, had Officer Smith's ship not been hovering right above us.

Diagnostic readings appeared on my monitors.

"I can't see any malfunction," Smith's voice said. "You wouldn't be lying to an officer of the law now, would you?" A melodic trill followed his words, as his computer processed our ship. "And I see you've already got two citations in this system. Guess this would be ticket number three, then. Which means we have to impound this fine vessel." There was no hiding the amusement in his voice.

Bastard. I considered explaining, but who would believe me? The Mark Nine was impervious to hackers. I had said so myself, not a moment ago. *Damn you, Mr. high-and-mighty Techsmith!* I swallowed to clear the rasp in my voice. "Officer, I swear, I don't know what happened. One moment I was in subspace, the next I found myself in normal space."

"I understand," he said with mock sympathy. "Why not explain that to the judge? In the meantime, let me update this for you."

In front of my eyes, the big, red number two blinked momentarily before transforming into a cheeky three. *No, no, no, no, no!* I banged my fist against the display.

"Your ship details have been noted," Smith continued gleefully. "Please contact the impound authorities at the Alpheratz station as soon as your"—he chuckled—"*technical* problems are solved. They've been notified of your arrival and will be awaiting you."

Just as abruptly as they had appeared, the red and blue lights disappeared in another blinding flash.

I let out a groan. The number three blinked on and off, as if mocking me. "You bastard!" I shouted at my passenger. I ran my hands through my hair. "This is all your fault. You're—"

He leaned back in his chair and placed his hands behind his head, a smug look on his face. "Chill, man. It's no big deal."

He sounded like a stoned twentieth-century surfer, which only made my blood reach boiling temperature. "No big deal?" I screamed. "What do you mean, no big deal? This was the perfect job for me. I'll be lucky if I'm allowed to test drive a garbage truck after this."

"Meh…"

He pushed his glasses up again, making me wish I could feed them to him. I ground my teeth.

"You see," he continued, "no copper in the universe can remember his own name, let alone your ship registration number, unless it's written down."

"How does that help me?" I said with a groan. "It's all in his computer by now."

"Why, yes," he agreed, bobbing his head up and down. "Yes it is."

The number three flickered and transformed back into a nice, glowing two, then a one, and finally a lovely, round zero. My gaze snapped to my passenger. "You…"

"Now, why don't you show me how fast this baby can *really* go? I bet you ten credits it can reach .05 in under twenty seconds."

My face broke out into a huge grin as I clutched the propulsion lever. "Twenty credits says .06."

He grabbed the armrest and smiled from ear to ear. "You're on."

For the Last Time!

Truth be told, I have no idea who built the damned contraption. All I know is that, if they were standing in front of me, I would have some choice words for them. Not that I don't appreciate the technical difficulties of a time machine, let alone one that can fit in a pocket. I'd simply want them to experience first-hand the mess that time travel is.

Perhaps I should start at the beginning, though. Which had me sitting on my battered sofa with the telly on, half-eaten pizza slice in hand. My astonished gaze was travelling from the scalding hot tomato stain on my t-shirt to the two copies of myself fighting in front of me. OK, perhaps even "astonished" can't begin to express my feelings. My eyes were about to pop out of their sockets and go to the sink to throw some water on them. They must have looked like Kermit the Frog's if he caught Miss Piggy in bed with a garter-wearing Gonzo.

Not that I blame myself. A moment ago I was watching the telly, and now, following two almost simultaneous blinding flashes that made the room look like an x-ray of itself, I was watching a rather unique sight. One copy of me, featuring a black eye and a torn t-shirt, was yelling some nonsense about bouncing mothers of snakes or something and was pointing towards the silver do-thingy another copy of me was holding. That second copy looked sharp, like he had just stepped out of the shower, and was wearing freshly ironed clothes. He was gaping at the yelling version of me—or should I say, us?—with a perplexed look on his face. A feeling I shared completely. Therefore, when he threw me the silver thingy and shouted "Just press the button", it was inevitable that I would listen to him instead of the manic version of me.

What the clean version of me failed to mention was the shock of traveling from one time-space continuum to another. It's like your brain performs a toe loop inside your head, followed by the entire universe. In simple terms, awful. And it leaves the worst hangover imaginable to man; something akin to waking up to municipality workers outside your window, operating the loudest drills available to public servants, after a week of drinking. Like I said, awful.

As soon as the pain dulled down a bit and the workers went for coffee and donuts, I opened my eyes. I was sitting on my sofa, the huge red stain on my t-shirt staring up at me accusingly. The sofa expressed its displeasure at having my not insignificant weight suddenly materialize on it with a loud groan. I raised myself with an equally loud grunt and looked around. I was still in the living room. The TV was switched off, while a small pack of newspapers covered the coffee table before me. That wasn't strange in itself; I always bought at least three newspapers over the weekend and spent the entire week slowly reading through them, until I had sucked any useful information or gossip out of them.

The strange thing was that it was a Friday when all of this happened, so the table should be empty. I leaned slowly forward to pick the top one up and a worker in my head remembered he had left his job unfinished and returned for a quick bash with a giant hammer. Letting out a heartfelt moan, I looked at the front page. I had no idea what events the newspaper was referring to, so my eyes started a casual stroll that ended up at the date. Which was nine days after today.

After the initial shock (significantly minor compared to the one I had already experienced), my eyes rolled back down to stare at my hand, still holding the do-thingy. The contraption looked simple enough; a surprisingly smooth silver rod with no obvious opening for batteries or something. It sported two round dials, a big button that I had already pressed once, and two small displays with numbers on them. They seemed familiar, and looking at my watch I realized the top one was the date and the bottom one the time. I already knew what the button did and decided to let it be for now, so I fiddled with the dials, discovering I could make the displays change by turning them. If that accomplished what I think it did, I could go anywhere – or, more precisely, any time – I wanted!

I would like to see what anyone would do in my place. For a short while, I glanced back and forth between the thingy and the pile of newspapers. Then—and I'm ashamed to admit this—the first thing that came through my mind was to check out the lottery numbers. I know it should have been something better. Something that would allow me to prevent some horrible accident; to save dragons in mortal danger from mad princesses or something. And yet, all I did was jot down six numbers on a piece of paper and stuff it into my pocket, as if this was a dream and I might wake up any moment. If there were any dragons in peril, they never had a chance as I dialed the numbers with trembling hands and selected the date before the next big jackpot. Then, closing my eyes, I pressed the button.

I wish I could say that the trip got easier the second time. It didn't. The dull pain in my head seemed to meet up with the new, sharp one and immediately hit it off, the way really annoying people do. They seemed to invite a couple of friends to throw a wild party inside my head. And yet, none of this mattered. I found myself back on the sofa with nothing changed around me, save for the pile of newspapers that had vanished from the table. I dashed to the door, ignoring the momentarily blinding pain, pausing only to grasp some change from the box next to it. Then, I scrammed like a madman to the betting place, holding the small piece of paper like a sacred relic in my hands.

The many pains in my head were now singing drunkenly, "If I were a rich man", from *Fiddler on the Roof*, but even that failed to bother me. All I could think of was how to spend the time until tomorrow's draw, and whether it would be worth using the gadget to save me some waiting hours. In the end, it occurred to me I had another trip to make first, so I headed into the shower instead.

I was stepping out of the bathroom, drying my hair with a towel, when I heard someone at the door. It dawned on me that I was sharing that timeline with another version of me, one that I was not ready to meet yet. I ducked in panic behind the sofa just as the door swung open. One quick look revealed the visitor to be my mother. She was dressed up funnily, as if she had thrown on the first thing she could find on her way out, and had a worried look on her face. I had no idea what she was doing so early at my place, and watched in wonder as she grabbed some clothes and stashed them into a bag. I almost jumped out to ask her what she was doing, but then thought better of it and stayed put.

She was now collecting some underwear, murmuring something under her breath, and I was reminded of all the times she would go after me, checking after my underwear.

"Come on, no-one's gonna see them anyway," I would reply, trying to get her off my back.

"What if you're run over by a bus, what will the doctors say?" she would ask accusingly.

Seriously, as if I'd be lying on a hospital bed covered in plaster from head to toe, leg hanging from the ceiling, with a doctor holding my clothes and telling her off with a stern voice: "He's in critical condition, but never mind that now. What I really wanted to discuss with you, ma'am, is the state of his underwear. This is a *disgrace*; how could you let him leave the house like that?"

Anyway, her current behavior did not make much more sense to me. Still, I preferred to lie quiet, in the safety of my hiding hole behind the sofa. What if another me was to step into the house just as I emerged? That would take some explaining—and I could hardly figure out what was happening myself!

Mercifully, she seemed to have other plans for the evening, so she performed one of her trademark sighs-with-simultaneous-rolling-of-the-eyes and stormed out of the house, slamming the door behind her. I executed one of *my* trademark sighs-with-simultaneous-rolling-of-the-eyes and emerged from behind the sofa. It let out another loud groan as I jumped on it and switched on the TV. She had left just in time; the lottery was about to begin.

I was nervous as a long-tailed cat in a room full of rocking chairs and my eyes kept darting towards the door. Then, the winning numbers appeared on screen and I couldn't care less if Dumbo the elephant waltzed in to tango with Cinderella. I kept glancing from the screen to the slip in my hand and back, a big grin plastered on my face. I was rich; richer than I could ever imagine.

And yet, I could not shake this feeling that something was wrong. I felt numb instead of ecstatic. Could the small voice at the back of my head whispering how the whole thing was fixed and I had no chance of enjoying my riches be right? It didn't matter, of course; there was no chance of me returning the money. I started thinking what to do with my new-found gazillions and my head spun. My eye was caught by the thingy that had made it all possible and I jerked up as I remembered that I still had to give it to myself, or it's bye-bye money!

I dressed up and carefully turned the dials to when it had all started. I winced, knowing what would happen as I pressed the button. Sure enough, the various pains in my head renewed the party as new guests walked in, carrying even more drinks with them. I tried to ignore all that to gaze at myself, sitting on the sofa. The poor fool jumped in fright, sending a thick glob of tomato sauce to land on his t-shirt, creating the stain I had just got rid of.

I took advantage of his surprise to turn the dials to next week and was about to hand him the gadget when another version of me appeared. Damn, I had forgotten about *him*. He started shouting some gibberish and approached me threateningly. I tossed the thingy to myself sitting on the sofa. "Just press the button," I yelled.

As the sofa version of me disappeared in a flash, it occurred to me that I had no idea how to return to my own timeline. Simultaneously, the maniac coming at me cried out loudly and punched me in the eye. His other hand had grabbed me, tearing my t-shirt as I turned away. Out of the corner of my eye I caught a silver flash in his pocket, and then it hit me: that was my ticket out! As I fell, I grabbed the silver rod and slammed the button. I hadn't had a chance to see when it would take me, but it didn't matter; anywhere had to be better than this.

My head was now about to explode, as I found myself once again in the familiar living room, mercifully alone. A painful glance at the rod revealed that I was in luck: I had been transferred to no more than a few days after winning the lottery. I sank heavily on the sofa, rubbing my temples, to wait for the throbbing in my head to subside. I brought my hand to my eye, wondering what the hell Future Me was thinking, when I heard a brisk rap on the door.

The last thing I wanted was to see visitors and I ignored it, but the rap turned to a loud thumping. I yelled for them to stop. Hearing my voice, they started to bang on the door, until it swung open. All I wanted was to take a couple of aspirins and lie down. Instead, I faced two statues at the doorway. I don't mean that in a good way; they bore no resemblance to, say, Michelangelo's David. No, what I mean is that they were like two granite lumps standing there. They looked like a living proof of evolution, with nature saving for them the part of the missing link, bulging muscles trying to escape tight black t-shirts.

I gaped at them with my one good eye, trying to figure out what they wanted, which is why I failed at first to notice the man standing behind them, hands behind his back. When he opened his mouth, his voice reminded me of a snake slithering in the woods, claiming to be a fruit seller, specializing in apples.

"Hello," he said, and I cringed. "We are here to propose a professional collaboration."

"What sort of collaboration?" I murmured, still trying to take in the scene. As I looked at him it suddenly hit me who he reminded me of: an old Asterix character that had the uncanny ability to spread discord wherever he went. I tried to smell him to see if he smelled of fish, but the two living rocks in front of me were in the way. Anyway, his face was more like a lizard or a snake than a fish. "A simple one," he carried on. "You give us the money you won, and we'll let you live. We know you brought it here."

Was I stupid enough to have brought my millions home? That made no sense! I hoped they were wrong and put on my poker face, something quite easy as half my face was numb anyway. "You're wrong, it's not here. Just take anything you want and leave."

He shrugged. "It doesn't matter; if we can't find the

money, we'll take something else. Say, parts of your body. Until you tell us where the money is, of course. You don't really need all those fingers now, do you?" One bouncer grabbed my right hand and a small knife clicked in his huge hand. Cold sweat prickled out of every pore of my skin. "We've been watching you since you went to the bank to get the ransom," he continued.

"Ransom?" I blurted out.

"Sure, ransom. Don't play dumb with us, we're not the cops." He saw my empty stare and laughed a cruel laugh. "No, we're not the ones who have your mother. But don't you worry about her; you'd better worry about yourself right now."

The fine hairs at my back stood up in an age-old response meant to scare off the opponent. Of course, that had the same effect as a mute ant threatening a deaf elephant. My mind raced as I tried to figure out what to do. "Fine, you win. Let me get the money." Was that my voice? I had no idea why I had said that.

Snake-face smiled contentedly and licked his lips. "I knew you'd see sense," he said, motioning the statue next to me to release my hand. The missing link let out a disappointed growl. "Go with him," Snake-face ordered him as I turned towards the bedroom.

I removed the gadget from my pocket as calmly as I could and turned the dials—not easy to do when your hands are shaking.

"What's that?" the missing link growled next to me.

"Oh, nothing." I tried to sound casual. "Just a remote to unlock the safe."

My fingers paused, hovering over the dials. What could be a good time for me to travel to? Even if I could get away from these guys and their likes, they still had my mother. *I told you that money was bad news*, the small voice in my head whispered. I hate smug voices, especially when they're mine. Cursing softly, I decided to end this once and for all. I had to go back in time and prevent this whole mess. I hit the button and closed my eyes just as I heard Snake-face yell, "Stop him!" behind me.

The by now familiar headache was the least of my worries as I found myself back in the living room, staring at two more versions of me. I tried to figure out how to explain everything, and blurted out about my mom, the two bouncers and the snake-faced guy from Asterix, but stopped when I saw the way they were looking at me. I regret to say that I then panicked and went for the silver thingy. I thought I was quick as a flash, but the adrenaline made me not only quick, but also clumsy. I was shaking like a caffeinated leaf in a tornado.

As a result, the other me—that smug, clean one—had all the time in the world to throw the rod to the sofa-sitting one, staring at us like he had suffered a stroke. And yet, that idiot managed to hit the button just fine, disappearing with a flash and setting in motion this entire sad affair. "No!" I yelled, and punched the silly sod in the eye, pulling him towards me and accidentally ripping up his t-shirt. Damn, it was one of my favorites, too. I then remembered what had happened next and looked in my pocket for the thingy, which the smug me was now holding. The next flash saw him disappear from the room.

I was left alone, staring at the walls around me. I was broke, had no time-travelling thingy, and no idea what to do next. The whole thing made no sense, making me feel trapped inside a nightmare. All I wanted to do was wake up. I thought some fresh air might do me a world of good, and decided to go for a walk to clear my head, until I could figure out my next move. I tried to remember the lottery numbers, but had about as much luck as a dyslexic amnesiac with a stroke.

I stepped outside and onto the road, my mind frantic with thoughts. Which is why I never even saw the bus rushing at me.

The good news is that an ambulance was right behind the bus. The usual crowd of onlookers had a good look as the paramedics lifted me onto the stretcher. Except for the throbbing in my head, I could hardly feel my leg for the pain.

"It doesn't look too bad," said one paramedic. "Except

for the leg. It will probably need surgery."

"Sorry, mate," said the other one turning to me. "Looks like you're gonna be in the hospital for a while. Got anyone to bring you some clothes?"

I don't know if it was the pain or the drugs they were pumping into me, but the world was spinning around me as I gave them my mom's number. She would have to make the trip to the hospital a few times before I got out, but I felt a momentary sense of relief: I may have lost my money and the time machine, but at least she would be proud of me: I *was* wearing clean underwear...

A Note from the Author

These short stories were written in 2016, as a break from working on my epic fantasy series, *Pearseus*, and my third children's book, *Valiant Smile*. Much like the stories in my previous collections of short stories, they aim to poke holes at the fabric of reality, hopefully eliciting a chuckle or a shiver in the process.

Readers of my stories will have noticed my disdain for names, both for characters and places, whenever possible. This is because of my conviction that names inevitably restrict the reader's imagination. We all carry deep in our psyche an image for all names and places and this will necessarily carry on to the story, limiting the possible projections we can perform. I'd rather leave the canvas completely blank so that readers can color it any way they like.

About the Author

Nicholas Rossis lives to write and does so from his cottage on the edge of a magical forest in Athens, Greece. When not composing epic fantasies or short sci-fi stories, he chats with fans and colleagues, writes blog posts, walks his dog, and enjoys the antics of his baby daughter and two silly cats, all of whom claim his lap as home.

Nicholas is all around the Internet, but the best place to connect with him would be on his blog, http://nicholasrossis.me/

You can check out his books on Amazon:

http://nicholasrossis.com/rd?id=41

Acknowledgments

They say that everyone has a book in them. What they don't say is how much it helps if you're not alone in your attempts to share your words with the world.

Many thanks to my excellent editor, Lorelei Logsdon; my friends and beta-readers MMJaye, Michelle Proulx, Effrosyni Moschoudi and Don Masenzio, as well as all my wonderful ARC reviewers and friends.

A special thanks to the new friends I've made on social media, and to my readers—this endeavor would be meaningless without you. And a very special thanks to my fiercest critic and greatest help, my wife Electra.

Further Notes

If you wish to report a typo or have reviewed this book on Amazon, please email *info@nicholasrossis.com* with the word "review" on the subject line, to receive free bonus material.

Thank you for taking the time to read *You're in for a Ride*. If you enjoyed it, please tell your friends or post a short review on Amazon. Word of mouth is an author's best friend and much appreciated.

For every new review, my dog does a happy dance!

Continue reading with *The Power of Six: 6+1 Science Fiction Short Stories*, now available on Amazon:

http://nicholasrossis.com/rd?id=5

Printed in Poland
by Amazon Fulfillment
Poland Sp. z o.o., Wrocław